Pam's fear of bad omens colors how she sees everything that happens.

Mac glanced back at the young widow. Fine yellow hair concealed Mrs. Danner's face, her head bent as if in prayer. Her fingers knit together. Water-filled blue orbs appeared and stared back at him.

"Mr. MacKenneth. . ."

"Mac," he corrected.

"Mac," she continued. "You'll probably think less of me than you do already, but you seem to be a bad omen. Every time you appear, something bad happens. And personally, I've faced enough hardships. I don't want to risk more."

Mac mentally picked his jaw up from the floor, clamping his mouth shut so he wouldn't speak a word out of turn.

"Quinton died shortly after you arrived. Jasper showed up on the trail; and since you've returned, I've been shot at. Don't you think that's more than coincidence?"

Lord, give me the right words here. I don't want to alienate this woman further. "There is another side to what you've presented."

"What's that?" Her eyes searched his as if longing to be proven wrong.

Slowly he made his way over to her as if approaching a fawn. "God may have had me there to help you just when you needed it."

She blinked.

LYNN A. COLEMAN was raised on Martha's Vineyard and now calls Miami, Florida, home. She has three grown children and seven grandchildren. She is a minister's wife who writes to the Lord's glory through the various means of articles, short stories, and a Web site. She also hosts an inspirational romance writing workshop on the Internet and serves as advisor of the American Christian Romance Writers organization. Visit her Web page at: *www.lynncoleman.com*

Books by Lynn A. Coleman

HEARTSONG PRESENTS

HP314—Sea Escape
HP396—A Time to Embrace
HP425—Mustering Courage
HP443—Lizzy's Hope
HP451—Southern Treasures
HP471—One Man's Honor
HP506—Cords of Love

Raining Fire

Lynn A. Coleman

Heartsong Presents

To my grandson, Matthew, who's been slow to speak but from whom I expect great things will come.

A note from the author:
I love to hear from my readers! You may correspond with me by writing:

> **Lynn A. Coleman**
> **Author Relations**
> **PO Box 719**
> **Uhrichsville, OH 44683**

ISBN 1-58660-685-9

RAINING FIRE

Raining
Fire

Note to Readers:

On November 13, 1833, one of the greatest meteor storms ever seen played out in the sky over most of North America. The mountain men referred to this as "The Year It Rained Fire." During the four hours prior to dawn, thousands of meteors lit up the sky every minute, and the smell of sulfur hung in the air. Newspapers of that era reported that almost no one was unaware of the shower. If they were not alerted by the cries of excited neighbors, they were usually awakened by flashes of light cast into normally dark bedrooms by the fireballs.

This meteor shower was caused by debris from the comet Tempel-Tuttle, which travels our inner solar system on a thirty-three-year journey around the sun. The storm marked the discovery of the annual Leonids meteor shower.

one

November 1833
Cumberland Gap, Kentucky

"Quinton!" Pam Danner screamed, tumbling down the steep road through the Cumberland Gap. Pinned by the wagon against a huge boulder, Quinton appeared lifeless. Again she tumbled, tripping over the hem of her dress. Her fine high-heeled boots were no match for this rugged terrain. *I should have listened to Quinton and purchased a pair of traveling boots.*

One large wheel sat in his lap and crushed his chest against the stone. "Quinton!" she screamed again, finally reaching him. His eyes fluttered open, then immediately closed. "Dear God, help me." She pulled at the wagon. It wouldn't budge. *Leverage.* She scanned the area. Spotting a large, fairly straight branch along the side of the trail, she retrieved it.

"Hang on, Quinton," she panted. His eyes barely moved under their lids. "Dear God, no. You can't take him away, too." Tears burned the corners of her eyes.

A small trickle of blood edged his pale lips.

She pushed and pulled at a small boulder to bring it close to the wagon. Even if she did manage to lift the wagon, she couldn't pull him out. "God, help me!" She wiped the tears from her cheeks, placed the oak branch under the wheel, and wedged it across the smaller boulder.

"Stop," a deep voice hollered from behind. She turned to discover a bear of a man dressed in leather with a Kentucky

7

long rifle in his hand. "You'll kill him for certain."

Her hands released the pole as if it were on fire. He leaned his rifle beside the huge boulder and bent down to check Quinton's pulse. "He's alive but just barely. I'll lift the wagon; you grab him." He didn't wait for her reply.

She scurried into place.

He planted his feet. His face darkened as he lifted. "Now," he said in a strained voice.

She wrapped her arms under Quinton's and pulled him away from his trap.

The man released his hold on the corner of the uncovered wagon, and it immediately lunged forward. The iron-covered wheel scraped against the rock. The huge man bent over, maneuvering his hands around Quinton's still body. "Isn't good. He's busted up pretty bad. I suspect he's bleedin' on the inside. It isn't safe to move him. Whatever were you thinking, trying to drive a wagon over the gap?"

"We didn't. We took it apart and brought it over piece by piece. Quinton was working on the left wheel when it pinned him."

The man shook his head and stood up.

"You best make camp tonight. You aren't going anywhere." His gazed worked its way up and down the trail. "Where are your horses?"

"Quinton tethered them down a ways. He figured they could feed while he worked."

He nodded. Thick black hair spilled out of his coonskin cap. All the sketches she'd seen over the years of Daniel Boone and the other frontier men were rolled into this one man. "I'll fetch 'em, if they haven't been stolen."

"Stolen?"

"Bandits, Ma'am." He grabbed his rifle and ran down the mountain.

Quinton groaned.

"Quint, Quint. Please don't die on me."

"Pamela. . ." His lips shaped her name more than she heard his voice. Trembling, she leaned over him, wanting to touch him but afraid to.

"Hurts bad," he gasped, his breathing ragged and labored.

Carefully, she wrapped her hand around his. His response was nonexistent. She squeezed a little tighter. "Quinton, fight it. I can't lose you. I can't. I just can't."

"The store," he coughed. Blood spilled over his lips. Her stomach knotted. *Dear God, don't do this. Not now, not again.*

"Remember," he wheezed.

Remember? How could she ever forget? She hadn't wanted to come. She'd fought God, fought her parents, and had even fought Quinton. In the end she'd ignored all the omens and come anyway.

Now look what's happened. Quinton lying by a rock in the middle of nowhere, dying. She should have made him see that her parents' death was a warning to stay away from this cursed land. Angus, the old house slave, had warned her how things would be if they chose to move west. He said the air didn't smell right, that trouble was in the wind. She'd never understood how Angus would know all these things, but somehow he'd always been right. Or at least it seemed he was right more times than not. Her parents hadn't believed in Angus, and look where it got them. Dead. Quinton hadn't heeded Angus's warnings. Now he was dying, too.

"The dream," he sputtered.

It wasn't her dream. She'd wanted to stay in Virginia. Stay among her friends, society. She had no interest in taming the wilderness.

He squeezed her hand ever so slightly.

"Quint, I can't. I don't want it like you and Mother and

Father. I only came with you because you said I must. I can't go on without you."

His eyelids drifted shut. Slowly, he tried to raise them again.

"Quinton, please don't leave me." Tears dripped from her chin. Lovingly, she wiped them from Quinton's tortured face. She kissed his forehead and ran to the edge of the woods. "God, forgive me, I can't watch him die."

❧

Mac stroked the muzzle of the lead horse. Thankfully, they were still tethered where Quinton had left them. November brought far less traffic on the Wilderness Road. The drovers had come and gone earlier in the fall, bringing the herds of livestock back East to sell.

Not much hope for the young man. Perhaps he'd make it through the night and they could ride him in the morning to Yellow Creek. Nearest doctor was in Barbourville, but Mac doubted he'd make it that far. The young couple could spend the night in their precious wagon. Their supplies hadn't been restocked. It certainly wasn't going anywhere lodged up against Indian Rock.

Christian duty required him to help these poor folks. The eight-point buck he'd had in his sights moments before the squealing broke the woodland silence had bolted. He preferred deer to elk. Both were plentiful, and that eight-point buck was large enough to have met all his winter needs. But now he had neither deer nor elk. Instead he had a mess on his hands.

He tied the horses loosely to the wagon. A soft, golden hue filled the sky, the setting sun a sharp reminder of how little time they had before darkness enveloped the gap.

Gathering some standing deadwood and small stones, he lit a fire. "Excuse me, Ma'am," he called to the still distraught woman. "Sun's setting. We'll need to make camp."

She turned ever so slowly at the edge of the woods. Her golden hair hung haphazardly across her shoulders.

"We'll need to keep him warm." *Not that it would help much, other than provide the man a small bit of comfort,* he mused. *If he's aware of the heat at all.*

With deliberate steps, she plodded her way toward him.

"Let's make a bed in the wagon for you and your husband," he suggested.

She knitted her eyebrows, then nodded her head.

They really shouldn't move the injured man, Mac knew, but would it make any difference now?

"Pam," the wounded man moaned.

It was hard to figure why this woman didn't stay constantly by her husband's side. *It might be too painful,* he guessed.

She scuffled to her husband, bent over, and held his hand. Her hands trembled. Mac's gut tightened.

"Quinton!" The heart-wrenching plea echoed off the mountain.

Should he run to her rescue? Should he give them time alone? Uncertain, he sat on his haunches by the campfire he'd been making moments before.

She turned to Mac and motioned for him to come beside her. Tears slid down her cheeks. Mac obliged.

"Thank. . ." The young man coughed. His chest heaved from the heavy labor. "You," he finally managed to get out.

"No need, just doing what any good Christian would do."

The pale eyelids closed and opened again. *His agreement, no doubt.* The man's lips moved, but no words came. Mac bent down on one knee. Again the lips moved. Again, nothing.

Mac glanced over to the young woman who had buried her face in her hands, then leaned over again, his ear an inch from the dying man's mouth.

"Please, Pamela. . .safety. . ." The broken sentence whispered, then blazed a silent echo within his ears. *Take the woman to safety?* How could he argue with a dying man's request? He could bring her as far as the Cumberland Ford Camp. She could work for one of the taverns. Or, he supposed, he could take her to Barbourville.

"Creelsboro." The word barely escaped.

Mac wanted to plead with the man to fight, fight harder. But he'd been in this situation before. He knew the dying person was far more aware of his passing than those who stood around.

"Help, please." Another labored whisper passed.

The man's hand clutched his.

To bring a woman halfway across the state was a heap more to ask than for him to simply bring her to a nearby settlement or town. But he couldn't ignore a dying man's request. Not to mention, if his parents ever heard he'd failed to help a stranger, he'd be hauled off to the barn as if he were a child in need of correction from his father's broad leather strap. Nope, everything in Mac screamed to help, and everything in him feared lending a hand to this woman.

"I'll take her."

The waning clasp on his hand released. Quinton's gaze locked onto Mac's.

"I promise, her honor is safe with me," Mac reassured the dying man.

The man's lids opened and closed once more. Then the pale blue eyes focused past Mac toward the heavens. They widened, then immediately darkened. The final gasp of air escaped from his body. He was a young man who accepted death with a gentle peace, a calming peace. A peace that only God could give.

Mac reached over and closed the man's eyelids. *Father God, be with his widow,* he prayed.

⁂

Pamela prepared her brother's body for burial, washing his face and hands, combing his hair. Mac, as she'd learned the stranger's name was when they'd exchanged introductions, informed her they could take Quinton into Yellow Creek and bury him. Up here in the gap, solid rock lay six inches or less below the surface. She'd prepared her parents' bodies last year, a ritual all too familiar. She never would have dreamed she'd be doing the same for Quinton.

Darkness covered the mountain, a fitting end to Quinton's life. Mac, with his Daniel Boone attire, was a man of few words. Truthfully, she didn't feel like talking. She didn't want to eat, sleep, walk, or do anything. Getting Quinton's body ready for burial seemed logical, and doing something seemed far more practical than crying.

At least that's what she kept telling herself.

Mac said they'd put Quinton's wrapped body in the open wagon to protect it from the animals. She laid a cloth over Quinton's face.

"I'll carry him to the wagon," Mac whispered.

The gentle giant lifted the lifeless form of her brother. *What am I going to do now?* The thought of heading back East and the day-long prospect of carrying the wagon piece by piece over the gap again didn't interest her at all. But the dream of going farther west had never been hers. It had been the dream of her father, her brother, and even her mother, but never her own.

Mac returned to the fire and held a cup out for her. "Drink this."

"Thank you, but I'm not hungry."

"I don't blame you, but this tea will help you sleep tonight."

"What's in it?"

"Black cohash."

A female herb? What's this man doing traveling with that? Who is he? "Thank you." She reached for the cup and brought it to her lips. The tealeaves sat on the bottom of the cup as the warm liquid soothed her parched lips and mouth. She closed her eyes and sighed. Life. It didn't seem fair. Why was she alive and the rest of her family gone?

"Try not to think about it." Mac's gentle words broke her thoughts.

How could he know what I was thinking?

He sat down beside the fire.

"Why are you here?" she quietly asked.

A disarming grin creased his face. Several days' growth formed a shadowy beard. "I was hunting nearby and heard the accident."

"But why are you still here?"

"It wouldn't be right for a man to leave a woman alone, and I promised your husband I'd take you to Creelsboro."

"Quinton was. . ." Her words caught in her throat. Should she correct the man, or should she simply !et him believe she was a widow? Posing as a grieving widow would give her a bit more safety with this stranger, she decided. "How? When?"

"Those were his dying words, Ma'am."

She ran her finger across the rim of the tin cup. "I'm not certain I wish to go to Creelsboro."

"Why were you heading out there?"

"My father purchased a business a little over a year ago. Shortly after that, he passed on. Quinton was going to complete his dream."

He poked at the fire with a stick, stopped, then looked at her. Inhaling deeply, he continued. "I'm not one to disregard a dying man's wish, but if you don't want to go to Creelsboro, I'd be happy to escort you back East."

"I don't know if I want to return to Virginia, either." She

rubbed her temples. The whole prospect of deciding one's future when your family, your past, had just died seemed pointless.

"Tomorrow we'll go to Yellow Creek and take care of your husband's burial. I'll leave you there for the night with some friends. I'll return the next day, and perhaps by then you'll have a clearer understanding of where you'd like to go. But for now, it's time to sleep."

He stood up and held out his hand. Did he wish for her to sleep with him? Fear crept down her spine. "I'm not ready for sleep." A yawn betrayed her words.

"I set a bedroll by the fire for you. It won't be as warm as your wagon, but you'll be safe by the fire."

She tilted her head slightly to the right and saw the laid-out bedroll of woolen blankets. She swallowed hard. "Where are you going to sleep?"

two

Mac stood and stretched. As Mrs. Danner slept by the fire, he had kept watch throughout the night, taking in brief snippets of sleep. He gazed over at Indian Rock and groaned. What had he gotten himself into, making such a promise to a dying man? Fortunately he knew where Creelsboro was. His parents' farm was in Jamestown, a short distance north. Creelsboro was a boomtown of activity. Folks would load up on supplies there before they ventured farther west. He looked over to the sleeping Mrs. Danner and wondered what she could possibly do there, now that her husband was gone.

He rolled his shoulders. A man keeps his word, he resolved. He set his coonskin cap on his head and looked at the eastern horizon. A thin ribbon of pale yellow lit the saddle, the lowest part of the Cumberland Gap. He glanced back at Indian Rock. How many people had lost their lives due to this boulder? In years past, the Indians would hide behind it and ambush the parties coming over the saddle. Today, Indians hiding behind the rock weren't a problem. But who'd ever expect it to be a part of another man's death? He wagged his head and headed into the forest.

Bandits were a constant threat along the trail. He needed to be on his guard. A defenseless female alone on the trail would be an easy target.

Crack.

A small branch snapped. Mac knelt down behind a bush. He focused in the direction of the sound. He sniffed the air. Silence. *Too quiet,* he reasoned. He looked back at the small fire and saw the sleeping form of Mrs. Danner. Easing his gun off his shoulder, Mac readied it.

A small fawn came into view. Mac eased out a pent-up breath. The wind stirred the tops of the trees. *Father, keep me calm. We've got a long journey ahead of us. I'll need sleep.*

A sliver of the sun now radiated over the saddle of the mountain gap. He finished scouting the area and returned to camp. Perhaps he could get in an hour's sleep before the Widow Danner rose.

He went back to the fire and stirred the dying embers, putting on a pot for hot water and coffee.

Pamela sat upright and blinked. "Is it morning?"

"Getting there. There's a small spring to your right. It's not much, but it's enough to help you clean up."

She opened her mouth, then snapped it shut and nodded her head. Perhaps it wasn't right for a man to tell a woman she needed to clean up. Mac held down a grin, but the situation was humorous.

He watched her trek over to the pile of her belongings. Mac groaned. He'd have to pack the wagon. The Danners had more stuff than he'd ever seen anyone bring through the gap. It was probably a good thing they were traveling this late in the year. The mud would have slowed them down. Still, it would be a chore getting it over the Cumberland River around Flatlick. The crossing at Camp Ford wouldn't be too costly. That would be a blessing.

He surveyed their trunks and the mounds of items they had neatly packed on the side of the road. *How'd they ever get all of that in there?* he wondered. *Mrs. Danner will have to decide what comes and what stays.*

"Mr. Mac? What is your last name?" Pamela asked as she approached.

"MacKenneth. I go by Mac."

"Oh, I just assumed your first name was Mac."

"No, my first name is Nash, Nash Oakley MacKenneth, but everyone calls me Mac."

She nodded. "I'll fix us some breakfast. Shall we load the wagon after that?"

Mac sat down beside the fire. Widow Danner set a cast-iron frying pan on the hot coals. "I was just thinking about that. I'm not quite sure how you managed to get all of those items in that wagon. But some will have to remain behind."

She glanced back at the stockpile. "I wouldn't know where to begin. I suppose Quinton's chest could stay behind, although I'll want to take out his good suit for burial."

Mac scratched the nubs on his chin. *This could take all morning.*

A slab of ham sizzled in the hot skillet. Its fragrant aroma stirred his empty stomach.

She ran to a chest and removed a couple items wrapped in white linen. Upon her return, she flipped the ham over and produced a couple eggs that she proceeded to whip in a small bowl.

"You're traveling with eggs?"

"A farmer, a day's journey back, traded some fresh food for some of our supplies. They won't stay fresh much longer if I don't keep them in a cool stream at night. I forgot about them last night. . . ." Her words mumbled to an end.

"That's understandable."

She removed the slab of ham and set the whipped eggs in the pan, crumbling bits of cheese over them. He hadn't had a breakfast like this in months. *Perhaps taking her to Creelsboro won't be such a strain after all.* He fought back a grin.

"So, do you live around here?" she asked.

"I have a winter cabin a few miles south of the gap. During

the spring and summer, I live in Jamestown and help my parents with their farm."

"I'm sorry, I don't know much about Kentucky. Is Jamestown close by?"

"Actually, it's close to Creelsboro, and that's halfway across the state."

"Oh." Her hand paused from forking the now-cooked eggs from the frying pan to his plate.

"Mrs. Danner, I promised your husband I'd take you there. You don't know me, and I can understand your fear, but with God as my witness, you can trust me."

She looked down at her lap, wringing her hands. "I shall try, Mr. MacKenneth. We should eat so we can get a move on this morning."

He took the offered plate from her. "Thank you." He bowed his head for prayer. "Father. . ." He heard her metal fork clank on the metal plate as if dropped. *She doesn't pray, Lord? Does she believe?* "Lord," he continued, "we ask for Your traveling mercies this morning, and I ask You to give Mrs. Danner peace during this time of grief. In Jesus' name. Amen."

"Amen," she whispered.

ã

Making breakfast for Mr. MacKenneth seemed like the logical thing to do. Eating, however, took all her willpower. And praying? She struggled down a piece of ham. Praying was useless. She glanced over at her rescuer gulping down his meal. Being alone with a stranger in the middle of nowhere didn't ease the growing knot in her stomach.

Just yesterday. Was it really only yesterday she and Quinton had been talking about all the plans they had for the store? Stopping at farmers' homes gave them a pretty good idea of the standard items needed by those living in the area. But Creelsboro was more of a town for those heading farther west. They both had agreed they didn't know enough about Creelsboro and the surrounding towns to decide if local items would help the store grow. But a certain amount of bartering with the local farmers would keep them fed. They wouldn't have time to tend to their own livestock. Perhaps a couple chickens, but a cow and other animals would take up valuable space that would be needed for storing supplies.

Quinton was gone now. All the choices and decisions would have to be made by her. If folks would let her. How many men would trust a woman as the owner of a general store? Not many, she feared. *Lord, I don't know what to do.*

Pamela left her half-eaten breakfast and went through her brother's belongings. She removed a couple mementoes she wanted to save as keepsakes and a few that had belonged to her father. Leaving Quinton's chest behind wasn't enough. She would have to give up something else.

"What did you decide?" Mac huffed, having returned for another crate to be placed in the wagon.

"His chest can stay behind. I'll place these things in mine. The rest of these are items for the store. I have no idea what I can afford to part with."

She eyed her father's chest. It held the linens and, hidden in the bottom, their entire family assets. Mac had asked her to trust him, but the amount of money in there could turn the most honest of men. No, she'd have to keep another secret from this man.

"What's in this one?" He pointed to a large crate.

"Plow blades."

"That can stay behind."

"But. . ." She wanted to protest. *Didn't he know how much those things cost?*

He scowled.

"Fine, it can stay behind. Since you already know what can

and can't go, you decide. These three are a must." She pointed out which three items she was referring to.

"I know this is hard, and I know you're sacrificing a fair amount of income, but unless you want to drag your husband's body behind the wagon—"

"Don't you dare speak to me like that! Who do you think you are?" She planted her hands on her hips. "I may not be a frontier woman, but I certainly know what's right and wrong. You don't treat the dead—"

He raised his hands in surrender. "I'm sorry, you're right."

"Fine," she huffed and went to the wagon, where she started shoving the crates in the best order. Quinton had showed her how to disburse the weight more evenly for the horses.

A few hours later, they had the wagon loaded. Quinton's wrapped body lay on top of the crates, and a secured tarp covered all. They were slowly working their way down the mountain. Mac walked beside the horses, helping them resist the urge to run down the steep path. Pamela walked behind the wagon, easing the burden by a hundred pounds. The horses snorted under the strain of all the weight. Perhaps she should have left more items behind.

The cool autumn air blew past, a welcome relief to her overheated body. If nothing else, the silent trek down the mountain gave her time to think. It wasn't proper for a woman to travel alone with a man. Perhaps she could hire some folks to escort them. Although, Mac did say there were bandits in the area. Who could she trust?

The wagon jerked as its rear wheel went over a small outcropping of rocks. If only Quinton had believed her. The signs were all there, saying they shouldn't go. At least that's what Angus had said the tealeaves revealed. Quinton hadn't given much thought to tealeaves and the like. He'd even argued that she, by believing such things, was hindering her faith. But who was right now, Angus or Quinton?

"You know, Lord, I'm having trouble believing in You. Ever since Mother and Father died, it's been a struggle. Now You've gone and taken Quinton away. What do You want from me? Angus and the others say, 'You've got to help yourself. God is good, and all that. But you've got to be aware of the other forces in the world and pay attention to them.' Quinton didn't believe in such, and look where it got him. I guess I'm reaching out and asking You one more time, are You what the Bible says, or is faith what Angus speaks of?"

The Twenty-third Psalm drifted into her mind. *"Yea, though I walk. . ."* Pam groaned. *Do You have to take everything so literally, Lord? I'm trying, I'm honestly trying to believe, to have faith. I wouldn't be talking with You if I wasn't trying. But You're not making it easy, Lord. Just so You're aware how I feel, that's all that matters at the moment.*

Pam listened for any additional reminders from Scripture and eased out her pent-up breath. "I'm walking, Lord, I'm walking."

❧

Mac heard Pamela mumbling, praying, he supposed. But where was her faith? Did she have one? She did say *amen* after their morning prayer over breakfast. Of course, some of the roughest men he knew would say *amen* while possessing less faith than an ant.

On the other hand, she could have simply been lost in her grief and not given the Lord much thought. He certainly had caught her crying more than once over the course of the morning. She claimed not to be a pioneer woman, and that was evident enough, but he sensed she could be a wild cougar guarding her young when pushed too far.

Whatever possessed me to say such cruel things about her husband's remains? And I'm questioning her relationship with God? No wonder she doesn't trust me. Lord, I promised a dying man, and You know I'm not one to go back on my word, but if You see fit to have me hook this gal up with a group heading west, please guide us to them.

He turned back and watched her stumble over the rough terrain. Roots and small washouts along the trail made for an uneven path. Hundreds of head of cattle, pigs, and sheep had tramped through this road months before. Herding animals didn't leave level paths. And her fancy eastern boots were for city life, not the frontier. For a reasonably intelligent woman, she definitely had some moments that made him wonder if anything worked in her pretty little head.

"Ugh," Mac groaned. What was he doing noticing her beauty? *She's a widow. You don't admire a widow. Or at least you shouldn't,* he reprimanded himself.

The team of horses snorted. "Whoa, boys. You're doing fine." He patted the white striped muzzle of the horse closest to him. "Fresh water is moments away." He couldn't blame the team; they were working hard. He'd need to brush them down and let them cool before they continued to Yellow Creek.

"What's the matter?" Pamela asked as she rounded the side of the wagon.

"The horses smell the fresh water. There's a nice spring down a hundred yards. They'll need a break. It's a good time for them. After they drink, we can ride and should make it to Yellow Creek by nightfall."

"I'll make you something to eat while the horses feed."

"Don't go to any trouble. I have some pemmican in my pack." He tapped the leather pouch on his hip.

"Pemmican?"

"It's dried meat and berries. Great for hunting trips."

"Oh." She stood for a moment and let the wagon proceed past her.

Maybe I should have taken her up on the offer, Lord. You

know I'm not much good with people. You're going to have to help me here.

"Whoa." He brought the horses to a halt. Making quick work of releasing them from their rigging, he led them to the stream to drink and began rubbing them down.

Mrs. Danner stood by the stream with her hand on her hip, paused for a moment, then sat down on a boulder and lifted her face to the sun. Her blond hair spilled from her bonnet, her skin shimmering like fine china. She didn't belong here. She definitely belonged in a fancy house with servants.

She glanced back at him. "Do you really think they need to be rubbed down so soon?"

"They could probably walk to Yellow Creek without a problem, but why risk it? They worked hard."

"True." She got up and went to the back of the wagon, returning a moment later with a couple of horse brushes. Without saying a word, she went straight to work on the other horse. He neighed in agreement.

"How long before we reach Creelsboro?" she asked.

"If the weather holds, possibly eight or nine days. Were you planning on going by wagon the entire trip?"

"I believe so. Quinton had the journey pretty well mapped out in his head. Why do you ask?"

"We could make better time traveling by water for a portion of the trip."

"By steamboat?"

"Canoe." He glanced back at the wagon. "With this load, it probably isn't an option."

"Perhaps I can sell some of my wares to the folks in Yellow Creek."

"Perhaps." There was a very small group of farmers living in that area. "Camp Ford and Barbourville might hold better opportunities."

"I was told that this region of Kentucky was wilderness."

Mac chuckled. "What one man calls wilderness might be a metropolis to another. All depends on where a man's from and what he's used to. Me, I prefer far less souls. Too much like a city, if you ask me."

A horse neighed behind them. Mac reached for his rifle.

three

Pamela's hands froze over the rib cage of her horse.

"Howdy," Mac called out to the unwelcome guests.

"That your stuff up on the road apiece?" the stranger asked.

She couldn't see who it was or how many. Could they be the bandits? Fear gripped her backbone like a vise, applying pressure to the point she feared the slightest move would cause her back to snap in two.

"Afraid so. I hope to retrieve it later tonight. Why do you ask?"

"No reason, just curious." Leather creaked as the man descended from his horse.

Mac laid his rifle across his left arm with his right hand poised over the trigger guard.

"Whoa, Mac, it's me, Jasper. Got hitched? I thought you were a loner." Pamela eyed the disheveled man. His stomach hung over his belt and jiggled as he walked.

"I am, but you know the long winter can be cold and lonely." Pam wasn't too pleased to hear Mac's insinuation, but she also noticed he hadn't let his guard down. His finger remained snug against the trigger. For whatever reason, this Jasper was a man Mac didn't trust.

"She's a pretty little thing. Where'd you find her? In church?"

"She was praying the first time I laid eyes on her," Mac acknowledged.

Pam had to admit that was true. And he hadn't lied about them being married. Jasper just assumed. Who was this burly mountain man? Could she trust him?

"Hate to call the visit short, Jasper, but I promised the missus I'd get her to Yellow Creek before nightfall."

"Ain't no tavern there."

"True."

"Be happy to escort you. I'm heading that way," Jasper offered.

"Well now, Jasper, that's a mighty fine offer, but me and the missus. . ." Mac glanced over to her and winked. "Well, you know."

Jasper looked Pamela up, then down. She wanted to jump in the creek and cleanse herself from his slimy gaze. He slapped Mac on the back. "Never thought I'd see you hitched. See ya in Yellow Creek."

Pam noticed the strange weapon attached to his belt. It looked like a short handgun with a small handle and a barrel that was definitely shorter than usual, yet wide and thick. *If he isn't a bandit, he sure looks like one,* she mused.

Mac held up his hand, silencing her. He listened intently for a moment, then waved to Jasper as the man passed by.

"Who was he?" Pam whispered when Jasper had rounded the corner down the path.

"Trouble with a capital 'T.' It's never been proven, but I suspect he's one of the bandits I spoke of."

"What kind of a gun was that?" She came up beside Mac, who continued to watch the wooded area above the trail.

"An Artemus Wheeler. He got it in the navy. Nasty weapon. Can shoot six shots without reloading. All he has to do is spin those six barrels."

Pamela started to shake. Mac reached out and held her shoulders, pulling her close to him. "There's men in the woods watching," he whispered. "Jasper believes you're my wife. Forgive me."

She looked up to the tower of a man. "I appreciate the comfort, and I noticed you didn't lie. Jasper just assumed. You didn't correct his misconception."

"Thank you. I'd been thinking I'd drop you off at the Turners' farm, but I'm not certain I should leave you alone now. I suspect Jasper will be watching us for awhile."

"Why?"

"Why?" He helped her up onto the wagon. "Because a wagon this full is a temptation."

"Oh." She bit her lower lip to keep from exploding. *Why did life have to be so hard?*

Mac went straight to work hitching up the horses. *Hitched, what a rude term for marriage,* she thought.

The horses set, the wagon leaned to the right as Mac climbed aboard.

Late afternoon shadows darkened the trail. Lowering deeper into the valley, she remembered her brother's body lying in the wagon. She thought about his desire that she finish the dream—her parents' dream, her brother's dream, but never hers. Death circled around her like a vulture waiting for its next meal. Her gloom was compounded by fear—fear of the unknown, fear of the known, and fear that her relationship with God was but a wave of a feather away from dying, too. *How can I endure this, Lord?*

Every once in awhile she'd catch Mac scanning the hillsides. What did he see?

She wrapped her winter shawl over her shoulders and held it close to her chin.

"Yea, though I walk through the valley of the shadow of death, I will fear no evil," drummed in her head over and over with each passing hoofbeat. *Quoting Scripture couldn't hurt, could it?*

❧

On his left, Mac spotted some activity in the underbrush of

the trees. If he remembered correctly, they were about to turn a corner on the Wilderness Road. *A perfect place for an ambush,* he thought. He reached for his Kentucky long rifle.

Mrs. Danner seized his arm like a vise. "What's the matter?"

"Just being careful. I doubt anything will happen." *Please, Lord, keep us and her possessions safe.*

She nodded but continued clenching his arm. *Be awfully hard to shoot with her hanging on,* he mused. *Whoever was in the woods will be exposed soon. Or they'll stay behind,* he hoped. *It's more than likely Jasper's men continuing to keep watch.*

Mac scanned the western horizon. It would be nightfall by the time he and Mrs. Danner arrived at the Turners' farm. *Lord, prepare their hearts for our arrival.* They had a good barn and a large cabin. It would keep them safe from Jasper and anyone else who happened along. And Will Turner and his sons were none too shabby with their aim. Fact was, Will had been paid a few shillings for killing off some wolves in the early years of settling this part of Kentucky.

He caught a glimpse of Mrs. Danner nibbling her lower lip. "This here part of the Wilderness Road was first made by the Indians."

"Huh?"

"The Indians, they used to travel this part of the road for hunting. It's part of the original trail."

"Oh." She scanned the woods. "Are they gone?"

"The Indians are, and Jasper and his men soon will be. I think they're just watching, trying to decide if it's worth the trouble or not. You see, I have a small reputation in these parts."

She eyed him more cautiously.

"I'm a fair shot," he supplied for her benefit.

"Oh." She released her grasp of his arm. Hopefully he'd calmed her fears some and not created new ones. Perhaps he shouldn't have shared with her the thought that there might be danger. He could just as easily have said that black bears were known to be in the area. Which was true, and he wouldn't exactly be lying. He'd always prided himself on being a man of his word. How could one woman cause him to wonder if he shouldn't be quite so honest?

The wagon bounced over a small rock. "Sorry," he apologized. He wasn't used to driving a team of horses. His favorite modes of transportation were his feet and a canoe. As his backside began to protest his current form of travel, he felt certain he'd keep right on using those methods.

"I'm bringing you to William Turner's place. They have a good-sized cabin and a barn."

"Will they put us up?"

"More than likely. Out here everyone kind of looks out for everyone else." *At least the ones who are settlers.* She'd already learned about the others. He prayed she wouldn't experience their evil firsthand.

"How much longer?"

"Not too much. A couple miles and we should be able to see Will's farm."

She nodded.

She must still be working through the shock of her loss, he presumed. Then there was the fact that they were strangers, compounded by his natural tendency to be a loner. This was going to be a mighty long trek across Kentucky. He snapped the reins. "Yah, come on, boys. Let's get there before the sun goes down. Fresh oats are on me." *Providing Will has planted oats again this year.*

The valley spread before them. "See that smoke?" Mac pointed in the direction of the Turners' farm. "That's where we're headed."

Will Turner and his family had been busy this summer. The

rail fence extended farther along the edge of the road than the previous year. They hadn't turned more than twenty yards down the Turners' long path to their home when he spotted Will standing at the front door, rifle in hand.

"Howdy, Will. Mac here. I got a flatlander in need of a place to stay tonight."

Will set his rifle near the door and waved back. For a man in his early fifties, he stayed mighty fit. "You're always welcome, Mac."

"Whoa." He pulled back on the reins and brought the team to a halt.

Will's eyebrows rose, seeing a woman. "Hello, Miss. . ."

"Mrs. Danner," Mac introduced. "Her husband came by way of an accident. We'll need to bury him tomorrow."

"I'm sorry to hear of your loss, Ma'am. You're welcome to stay in the house. I'll have my wife, Mary, make a bed up for you."

"I don't mean to be any trouble."

"No trouble at all." Will smiled. "Mac, pull the wagon to the barn and take care of the horses. I'll be out shortly and give you a hand. Did you folks put a feedbag on?"

"Not since lunch. My stomach's been gurgling for a mile, smelling Mary's fine cooking."

Will chuckled. "We'll have a couple plates warm for ya. Excuse me."

Mac turned toward Mrs. Danner. "They're good folks. I think you'll enjoy getting to know Mary Turner."

"Let's get the horses brushed down before we lose all daylight," she suggested.

Mac placed his hand on hers. "Go inside, Mrs. Danner. I'll take care of the horses. I'll even bring your small bag in for you."

She looked down at his hand. He removed it. What was he

thinking? She gazed back into his eyes. "Thank you."

He assisted her graceful departure from the wagon. Mac swallowed hard. *She's beautiful, Lord. Guard me from any wayward thoughts.*

❧

Will and Mary Turner's home was simple but practical. The log cabin had several additions for each of their grown children and their wives. It was hard to believe all these people lived under one roof, but the house was set up in such a way that they each had their private spaces. A small room with a bed for guests made up Pamela's quarters. A wonderfully colored quilt covered the bed, and a fine feather pillow rested at its head. One wall was curtained with fabric. Behind it were all the canned vegetables the family had set up for winter. Even the small space under the bed doubled for storage.

A gentle knock on the doorframe caused Pamela to turn around. Mary Turner stood in the doorway.

"Are you all set, Dear?"

"Yes, thank you. This is very kind of you."

"No trouble at all. As you can see, we always have room for one more." Mary's smile revealed small wrinkles around her eyes, showing her age. She'd been the perfect hostess. She'd fed them, made them feel at home, and even provided Pamela with some water and soap to clean up with.

"Do you have guests often?"

"Not too much. Once in awhile we have a drover stay as he's heading back. But for the most part, it's pretty quiet these days."

"What's a drover?" Pam eyed the bed. Should she sit down or continue to stand? Knowing what to do in a stranger's house always left her with questions.

"They're the men who drive the livestock back East for sale. The biggest use of the road these days is from that of drovers. Most folks heading west are using different routes."

"Quinton said we would be traveling by ourselves most of the time."

"How did your Quinton pass on, if you don't mind me asking?"

Pamela sat down on the bed. Obviously her hostess wanted to talk, and Pam was glad to have someone to talk with. But as the image of Quinton squashed against the rock flashed through her mind, her hands trembled. Her lips quivered.

Mary Turner sat down beside her and wrapped her in a protective embrace. Odd, the woman had more muscle on her arms than Quinton had on his. Must come from working the land in the middle of nowhere.

"I don't know how it happened. One minute he'd nearly finished putting the wagon back together, and the next he was pinned between Indian Rock and a wagon wheel."

"Oh my, how tragic. I'm sorry. Have you been married long?"

Did she dare tell Mary Turner the truth? Tears welled in her eyes. She bit down on her inner cheek.

"Forgive me." Mary rose. "How'd you like a nice warm bath? I imagine it's been awhile since you've had one."

Pamela fought the desire to check her armpits and make sure she didn't smell.

Shock and worry crossed Mary's face. "Oh no, Child. I was thinking a warm bath comforts me. I don't get to take them often, mind you, but William built me a tub, and I've been spoiling myself every now and again. Might help relax you and work off some of the tension from traveling."

"It sounds heavenly, but I wouldn't want to put you to too much trouble."

"None at all. I'll get the menfolk to fill the tub." She winked.

Pamela had to admit she liked Mary Turner. Her kindness

equaled her very practical spirit.

Thirty minutes later, Pam found herself neck deep in warm water. She leaned her head back against the wooden tub. William Turner had done a fine job. She traced the wood grain with her finger. *I wonder if he'll take a trade,* she mused. *Nope, Mary would never part with it.* And she couldn't blame the woman.

A soft sigh escaped her lips.

"Feels good, doesn't it?" Mary said from behind the partition they'd put up around the tub. It really was quite an imposition. The men had to move the table, set up the tub, and fill it while Mary poured in the hot water she'd boiled on the stove. They told her they only took baths once a month. A girl could get used to this kind of spoiling.

"Mac, what are you doing back in here?" Mary's voice called out.

"I need to ask a favor, Mary."

Pamela wanted to hide. She heard Mary cutting and preparing something.

"Come on, Boy, spit it out."

"Can I leave Mrs. Danner with you?"

What? Pamela wanted to scream. *I thought he promised Quinton to take me to Creelsboro. Why has he changed his mind?* She couldn't stay here. The Turners were nice folk, and she could even see herself developing a friendship with them, but she wasn't a part of their family. She had no right to live here. *What is he thinking?*

"Does my Will know your reasons?"

four

"Yes." Mac heard water slosh from behind the divider. He still couldn't believe Mrs. Danner would be so brazen as to ask for a hot bath. He'd thought about not leaving her with the Turners for fear that she'd have them waiting on her. But if he was going to travel to Creelsboro, there were a few things he'd need for the journey back to his cabin.

"I'm fine with Mrs. Danner staying here if my Will is approving."

"Oh no, no. I didn't mean for her to stay a long time. I'll be gone for a day, two at the most. When I return, we'll continue on."

Mary nodded her head and wrung her hands off on a towel.

"Thank you." His gaze shifted from Mary to the folding partition. "Mrs. Danner, I'll be back to fetch you. Don't worry."

"All right." Her voice strained as if she wanted to say more. Their conversation had been limited. He'd given her space to grieve. He didn't know if fear of him or shock at her loss kept her tongue, but for a woman, she certainly used few words.

Mac set his coonskin cap on his head and left the farmhouse that had grown an additional room this past summer. Will was talking about building a new house with milled timber and two floors. He'd made a fair profit for the past two years and felt he could afford to have the chestnut trees on the back of his property milled.

Mac shook his head as he headed back down the Wilderness Road in a cloak of darkness. The moon was blanketed

35

with a cloud of lace as it stood half full, dancing off the ridge of Cumberland Mountain. He had no doubt that Jasper and his men had made camp someplace along the road Jasper would be expecting him to come back for the items they'd left at the saddle's ridge. Mac would have to remove some belongings and perhaps hide a chest or two in Gap Cave just north of the gap.

He kept an even pace that would allow him to run twenty miles in four hours. He'd make it home and still have enough time to rest before dawn.

The smell of a campfire alerted his senses. Someone was close by. Few camped these days, with all the folks who had opened their homes as taverns. So one had to be careful. He cocked his rifle and continued his pace. He had no objection to Jasper seeing him tonight. It would play well with the story he told.

A half mile past the campfire, Mac quieted his steps. His ability to blend in with the woodland areas gave him much success with hunting. Tonight it would serve him well in hearing if he had picked up a follower. He grinned. He'd picked up one man in relatively good shape. Mac kept his pace. This man wouldn't last long enough to make it up and over the gap. No, he was huffing too hard already. Mac would lose him before the gap, and his plan to store a chest in the cave would bode well for him. He'd open one chest and carry some of the clothing to his cabin. He prayed doing this would keep up the ruse for Jasper and his men.

Mac began the upward run toward the Cumberland Gap. His follower had slowed down considerably. When Mac arrived at Indian Rock, he found men's clothing hung haphazardly over the chests. Apparently Jasper and his men had already rummaged through them. He opened a large, sturdy shirt and piled other clothing on top of it. Using the arms and the tail of the shirt, he created a small bundle. He picked up the smallest chest and continued his run. Up and over the saddle, he worked his way and headed down the road. Just a little bit north was Gap Cave. After placing the chest in there, he strapped the clothing to his back and continued home. He prayed that his follower hadn't seen him working his way up to the cave. Thankfully the night sky shrouded him.

His undisturbed cabin greeted him as a welcome relief. He folded the clothing and placed it on a chair in his room. *Father, I hope this will convince Jasper.* Will Turner had agreed to take a couple of his boys and carry the remaining chests to his home. Mac rubbed the back of his neck. He hadn't asked Mrs. Danner if she minded his giving away her husband's belongings. But then again, he hadn't wanted to remind her of the loss.

He still couldn't believe the woman had asked for a bath. Of all the self-centered things to do. She obviously came from a well-to-do family. Her clothing and the amount of belongings they'd been carrying on their journey west were numerous.

He grabbed a kettle. Water slowly poured from the wooden barrel. A hollow sound echoed from it when he tapped the side. Nearly empty. He'd have to fill it if he were staying. Their journey would take him two weeks if they met with no hazards. He could return within a week after that, he hoped. If they didn't have so much stuff for the store, they could make the trip in less time. He doubted she'd reduce any personal items. And how could he ask? Her family heritage was in that wagon, and she'd need all the comfort possible to keep her through the lonely nights of loss.

With the water heated on the woodstove, he made himself a cup of tea. "Lord, give me a good night's rest and help me understand this woman. You and I both know my history when it comes to the fairer sex, and I've come to terms with the fact that I'm meant to live alone. What I desire most from life is not what women want. And as pretty as Mrs. Danner is, I can't be having thoughts and feelings for her. She needs to mourn her husband's death. I'm certain there is another man out there who would like settling down and wearing fancy clothes." Mac yawned. "Forgive me, Lord, for carrying on here."

He finished off his tea and headed for bed.

His door rattled in its hinges.

❧

Pamela pulled the quilt up over her shoulders. It felt so good to sleep on a mattress again. For five days she'd been sleeping on the ground, dealing with bugs and vermin. *Goodness, Lord, why did Quinton insist on our going west? I know Father purchased the business in Creelsboro, but. . .* She rolled over and buried her head into the pillow. *No, I'm not going to think about this again. It's over. They're dead. Quinton's dead. Why do I have to go on to Creelsboro? Why do I have to go anywhere?*

Quinton's strained words came back. "Remember the dream."

She punched the pillow and closed her eyes tight. *It's not my dream. So why am I alive and not them?*

Reality stung.

❧

Sunlight streamed through the small window. It was morning, time to rise and time to face her brother's death. Today she would bury him. The Turners had given her permission to bury Quinton in their family plot.

Resolute, she flopped the covers off and dressed. It would take the better part of the morning for her to dig Quinton's grave.

"Good morning, Mary," she said to the kind woman with

broad hips and broad shoulders standing at the stove.

"Morning, Dear, have a seat. I'll serve you up some pancakes and eggs. How do you like yours cooked?"

"I can cook. You don't need to go to any trouble."

Mary continued to work at the stove. "No trouble at all. I always fix a big breakfast. Everyone will be in from early morning chores in a minute."

Pamela's stomach rumbled as the scent of fresh bacon filled her nostrils. On the table she found a plate of sausages, home fries, a stack of pancakes, a loaf of fresh bread, some bowls of various jams, and a jar of canned peaches. *Is she feeding an army?*

"Set yourself down. They'll be here in a minute or two. You haven't told me which way you like your eggs."

It was no longer a question. "Any way. I like them the way you're serving them."

Mary nodded her head, grabbed two more eggs from a bowl, and cracked them open over a flat grill. This was a working farm. Pamela had never been on a farm early in the morning. Some friends back East had told her how much work they would have to do before they ate breakfast and before they left for school. She'd always thought they were exaggerating. *Perhaps not,* she mused.

Pamela sat down, then realized they probably had an order. "Is there a particular place I should be sitting?"

"Nope, first come, first served here. It's my job to fix the morning meal. Lunch, every man, woman, and child fends for themselves. At dinner, each of us women takes a night. Whoever cooks doesn't clean."

Pamela chuckled. "Sounds wonderful."

"You need order when blending four families under one roof. We're hoping to build a new house next spring. Will Jr. and his family will stay in this house, and the rest of us will move into the large farmhouse. Eventually each of the boys wants to build their own homes. We'll apply for a tavern license then and hope to use the rooms for travelers like yourself."

"Seems like a lot of work."

"Always is when you're trying to build a community. The Cumberland Ford settlement just up the road is doing well. But it's taken them a few years. Most folks don't stop here at Yellow Creek. They just head on up to Cumberland Ford. Of course, most folks aren't hauling a wagon like yourself."

"It's not the most comfortable road."

"Ain't built for wagons. You shouldn't have too much trouble crossing at Flatlick. I heard they moved the tollgate down there in 1830. You could try crossing other places to avoid the tolls. Depends on how low the river is and how mucky the shoreline."

"Great," Pamela mumbled.

"If you don't mind me asking, what are you taking to Creelsboro?"

"Mostly things for the store. There were a few pieces I left up on the gap—some lamps, small furniture pieces. Most of those were in the large trunk."

"Will said he and the boys were going to fetch your trunks today."

Why? she wondered.

"Mac said you ran into Jasper, and he told Jasper he was going to go back for 'em. So he and Will figured the best thing was to fetch 'em."

"Well, you and your family can keep whatever you want from the trunks. Quinton's clothing was left behind. Didn't figure I'd be needing that." Pamela bowed her head.

"Speaking of Quinton, the boys ought to have his grave dug before breakfast."

"I was going to do that. I don't want to impose."

Mary came beside her with a platter full of fried eggs and placed her hand on Pam's shoulder. "Now, Dear, a woman shouldn't have to dig her husband's grave. It's been done, but my boys are strong, hardy men. They can do it in no time. You just rest. You've had quite a heap of trouble for one so young."

Pamela sighed. *Mary didn't know the half of it.*

The door flew open, and a team of people bustled into the room. Each grabbed a plate, filled it, and sat down. Pamela sat watching, holding her fork in midair. They weren't pushing or shoving, but they worked in pace with each other. A dance of sorts. A breakfast waltz. She shook her head. She'd been away from civilization too long, and it had only been five days.

The morning meal went by as quickly as it started. Pamela found herself alone at the table, the three other women standing at the sink, one washing, one drying, and one putting the dishes away. *Talk about an organized household.* The women chatted on and on about their plans for the day.

Mary came in from her private room with a clean house-dress on. "Takes some getting used to, doesn't it?" she asked as she sat down beside Pamela.

Pamela stared down at her half-full plate. "I've never seen a meal eaten so quickly yet orderly at the same time."

Mary roared. "A couple hours of hard work drives a person to not waste time." She placed her hand on Pamela's. "When you're ready, we'll bury your husband. Will thought it'd be fittin' to read the Twenty-third Psalm."

How'd they know that psalm has been running through my head for days? On the other hand, it was the standard Scripture to read at funerals. Even the preacher back home had read it at her parents' grave. Pamela cleared her throat. "That'll be fine."

"God's got big shoulders, Dear. He understands our tears and our anger."

Pamela eyed Mary cautiously.

"It's been a few years, but I remember crying out to the Lord over the loss of my young ones."

"I'm sorry."

"It still hurts when their birthdays come around, but I remind myself of all the hard times we've gone through and relax in knowin' they never knew pain, hardship, and anguish. They've only been held in the Lord's bosom."

Pamela noticed the chatter of the three other women had ceased. She looked up, realizing each of them had their own losses to bear as well. *Why, oh why, do people willingly want to live in such wilderness?*

❧

"Black Hawk, what are you doing here?" Mac opened the door wider and let his old Indian friend in.

"I am old. I wish to die with my ancestors." Black Hawk sat down on the bench by the table.

"But, if they catch you. . ."

"They will not catch me. See, I wear white man's clothes, and my hair is hidden under my cap."

Mac had never known Black Hawk to wear anything but his tribal clothing. He'd taken a risk to come back East. His people had been forced to move to Indian Territory years ago. But Black Hawk had always defied the "white man laws" and lived as he felt he should.

"My home is your home. I'm going to bed to rest. I'll be packing tomorrow, then heading west for a few weeks."

"What is this I hear about a woman?"

"You met up with Jasper?"

"No, I overheard them. Beware, my friend. His eyes are on you and your bride's wagon."

"She is not my bride." Mac's voice rose.

Black Hawk's eyebrows did likewise.

"Sorry. Jasper assumed she was my wife. She is a widow. Her husband died at Indian Rock two days ago."

"Ah, I saw the blood."

Mac had thought he'd cleaned the rock well enough. But for someone like Black Hawk, obviously not. "I promised her husband I would take her to Creelsboro before he died."

Black Hawk nodded. "Do as you must, but beware."

"I will, and before I leave I wish to have words with you."

"It will be my pleasure, Swift Deer." His leathery smile accented the deep wrinkles in his face. Black Hawk had taught Mac to hunt, to live off the land, and to identify plants that were helpful for medicine. He owed the man a debt of gratitude and a heap of prayers. As of yet, Black Hawk had not seen the white man's God as the answer. *If he's dying, this might be my last chance, Lord. Help me.*

"Good night," Mac said and smiled.

"You mean, 'good morning.' " Black Hawk chuckled under his breath.

"Yeah, nothing like being up most of the night. Let's get some rest, and we'll talk later."

"Swift Deer, your heart is still pure. It's your faith, I see it now."

Mac halted in his steps. He glanced back at Black Hawk. Unspoken words proclaimed the glory of eternity in the simple wink of an eye. Black Hawk had come to terms with the white man's God. *Thank You, Lord.*

After a gentle nod from Mac, Black Hawk laid a bedroll down in front of the woodstove, his movements stiff, his frame thin, thinner than it had been several years ago after he'd returned from Indian Territory. "Black Hawk, sleep in my bed tonight, please," Mac pleaded.

The old man looked down at the bedroll. "Thank you, my friend. My brother."

Mac swallowed a lump in his throat the size of a chestnut. He pulled a small pillow from the bench in the living room. His mother had made it for him last year. He stripped to the waist, removed his boots, and lay down on the hard floor. Black Hawk was a wise man and knew he was dying. *Father in heaven, forgive me. I don't want to fulfill a dying man's request. I'd rather stay by the side of my friend and help him exit his earthly home.*

five

Quinton's wrapped body lay silent and still in the bottom of a filled pit. The last bit of hope that all of this had been some strange nightmare took flight. Oh, how Pamela prayed to wake up in her old bed. Mary's warm embrace helped, a little. Tears streamed down her face. Will's kind words gave little solace. Quinton was dead. She was alone and condemned to live a dream that others had created.

Pamela gripped her sides as she held back some of her emotions. These godly people would not take too kindly to her spitting words of anger out to God. Granted, Mary had mentioned that God could handle it. But it slammed into everything she'd been taught. In church you learned to respect God and accept what He gave in life, whether it be good or bad. Her slaves told her not to anger the gods, to tread lightly.

"We'll leave you be for awhile, Child," Mary whispered in her ear. The family of strangers who had opened their home knew her pain. And they claimed God could handle her grief, her anger, her questions. Was it possible? Or was this a new brand of religion? Wilderness religion.

She'd been told only a half dozen farmers lived in the region of Yellow Creek. Most folks were in Cumberland Ford, where they could find a traveling preacher some days. Will and his sons had offered to see if they could find one to do the service. But Pamela insisted they not extend themselves further.

"Thank you," she whispered. *How can I ever repay this family for their kindness?* she wondered.

She turned and looked at the freshly dug grave. A single

45

tear plopped on the soil below. Her face felt swollen. Grief shook loose any restraints holding back the tears from the strangers around her. She could expend all her emotions now. Later, she'd be expected to be grown and mature, to have put the matter behind her. Hadn't that been what her father had always taught them with each death that overshadowed her family?

"God, why have You cursed us? What did my ancestors do to allow You to punish us for generations? When does it stop? When I'm dead and buried? Take me now, Lord. I don't want to go on. Why should I? It was never my dream. It was Yours. . . my parents. . .even Quinton's. But maybe he just felt it or thought it the best way to go.

"I know You don't care for those who speak with the spirit world. But Angus and the others said trouble would happen if we left Virginia. I'm sorry, God, if I'm not supposed to believe in such nonsense, but You've left me no choice. They were right. My family and their beliefs about You, about Your direction, were wrong. Look at them, they're all dead!"

Pamela's chest heaved. Her fist clenched, she raised it toward the sky. "Take me, God, take me now. I don't want to live without them. I'm alone. No one cares for me, not even You."

Fresh tears spilled down her cheeks.

A gentle breeze whispered across her heated flesh. A voice—no, the feeling of a Presence—swept over her, and the words from the Twenty-third Psalm passed through her mind. "Yea, though I walk through the valley of the shadow of death, I will fear no evil: for thou art with me; thy rod and thy staff they comfort me."

"Where are You, God? Where?" She looked around the expanse of the meadow, the rugged foothills climbing up to the mountains. "Are You up there? Down in the valley? Where are You, Lord? I can't see You. I can't feel You. I can't feel anything right now. I'm so empty, Lord. So completely empty."

Pamela crumpled to her knees, hunched over her brother's grave. *Evil is all around, Lord. Look at Jasper. And can I really trust that giant of a man, Mac?*

Thy rod and thy staff comfort me.

"Lord, I may not have paid attention as I should have in my church lessons, but isn't the rod used for discipline? For spanking children? I'm not a child," she huffed.

A man coughed. "Do you think it might be that it's because a parent loves his child that he disciplines him?"

Tear-soaked eyes blurred her vision. Pamela tried to focus on the image of Calvin Turner leaning against a shovel.

"Forgive me for overhearing, but if a young one keeps reaching for the hot stove, a parent needs to spank their hand to keep them from doing far worse damage to themselves. I know you're hurting, and your loss is great, but I've always found new life springs from death." He nodded and placed his molded woolen cap back on his head. "Fact is, bad things happen all the time. My young wife didn't deserve to die in childbirth, but she did. It wasn't God's fault. It wasn't my fault. It wasn't even my child's fault. Those things just happen from time to time. They hurt, they're unfortunate, but from her death new life came—my boy, Jason."

He bent down on one knee and picked up a small pebble. "She's still in my heart. I love her. I miss her. But God's also given me a new wife and a new child on the way. I'm not saying this is easy. Lord knows, I cried out to Him like you are doing on more than one occasion. I'm just saying that as bad as it feels right now, there will be a time when it won't ache as much. You might not understand all the reasons why, but you'll be comfortable with the fact that it's happened.

"Ma thought I might be able to help you deal with your anger, seein's how I'd been there, too."

Pamela swallowed hard. "I'm sorry for your loss." What else could she say?

He pointed to her left. "That's Catherine's grave."

"How long?" She wiped the tears from her eyes.

"Four years this past August. I ain't perfect. I still hurt. But as that psalm says, Thy rod and staff do comfort."

"What's God's staff?"

"To me it's like a staff a shepherd uses to tend the sheep. He'll nudge a lamb here and there with the tip to keep it on the right way, so as not to get caught in the briars or other things on the path. He also uses it to help him continue on the long miles of the journey. You know, somethin' to lean on. Just like this shovel." A lopsided grin slid up the right side of his face. His rugged chin and wayward hair showed he was content with who he was. He had no need to impress anyone. He simply lived his life out to the fullest.

Am I vain, Lord? she prayed. *Have I been trying to do it all my own way?*

⁂

Mac woke to find Black Hawk reaching over him to the woodstove.

"Sorry, Swift Deer, I did not mean to wake you, but my old belly was in need of something warm. The wind blows from the northwest. It will be a cold winter, lots of snow."

Black Hawk had never been wrong on his weather predictions. *I'll have to chop more wood for the winter,* Mac mused. The window brought in the warm rays of sunshine. And for the first time, he noticed how the creases in his old friend's forehead and cheeks were deeper, the luster of his eyes gone. Only dull orbs remained. Mac sat up.

Black Hawk took a seat on the bench. "The time is close."

"I'll stay with you."

"What of this young woman who needs you?"

"I'll send word, hire someone else to take her."

"Ah." He leaned back and rested his elbows behind him on the table. "I do not want you to go back on your word, my friend. Not for an old man who's lived too many days."

"Nonsense. You're not that old."

Black Hawk roared with laughter that lapsed into a chest-rattling cough. "Older than you are aware, my son."

Mac clasped his hands in front of him, resting his elbows on his raised knees. "When did you make peace with the white man's God?"

"Six moons ago, when a preacher came to the reservation. You know how fired up I was about being there. Well, he spoke about God's people, the, how you say, Jews, and how they were taken from their land, used as slaves, and one day their God rescued them and brought them back to their Promised Land. This is my land, my promised land. Your God, my God, brought me back so I can die on my land. The land of my people. A gift, you might say."

Mac searched his memory to see if he'd ever told the story of Moses to Black Hawk. He thought perhaps he had, but found no definite recollection.

"You, my friend, were an example of the life your God, my God—I have to learn to keep saying that—wants people to live. There is a lot of evil in this world. I see it in white man, red man, black man, every man I've come across. They lie, they cheat, they kill. But you, my friend, never, never in all my days of knowing you, did. Why? I'd ask myself. Then I'd remember your words about your God. When this preacher came, I chose to come and listen. Then it made sense.

"I'm old. I'm tired of fighting. I want to have my spirit rest on the wings of God."

"This is why I should stay," Mac protested. "I should be with you."

"No, my friend, you must keep your word. How shall I continue to believe if you do not?"

Mac wasn't too sure how he liked his life being an example that a man based his entire faith from. He pinched the bridge of his nose. "Then come with me. I could use a chaperone."

Black Hawk chuckled. "I said I understand your God. I did not say I understand your women. Why is she not married to you right now?"

"Her husband just died." Mac swallowed hard.

"Exactly. A woman needs a new husband to feel complete, to feel loved. A warrior takes on a widow to keep her content, to give her children if she is without. This makes a woman happy."

"I do not understand women, either, so I'll just let someone else make her feel loved and give her a child."

Black Hawk wagged his head. "Is she not pleasing to behold?"

"She's beautiful. But you know my past. I could never. . ."

Black Hawk raised his hand and held it out toward Mac. "I once said I could never believe in the white man's God. I do not think *never* is a good word. It isn't true."

Mac opened his mouth, then closed it. How could he argue with that kind of logic?

"Go, take this woman to Creelsboro or wherever you said she must go. And if she pleases you, make her your wife. Don't think. Just do what your heart is telling you. Wonders are found in the arms of the woman you love."

"I shall take the woman to Creelsboro, but I will not take her as my wife. She is grieving. And I like living alone. I have no woman to tell me what to do every day."

"And no woman to warm your bed."

Mac's cheeks flamed.

"Ah, my young friend. Forgive. Anger only dries up the

spirit of the white man's God who lives within."

Mac blinked at Black Hawk. How could he be so wise and have known the Lord for so little time? "Please come with me. I wish to spend these last days with you."

"I would like that, too. But I am to die here. It would be a risk for me to travel by day."

True, he'd be sent back to Indian Territory. Or be killed trying to resist capture. "All right then. You can make yourself comfortable in my home."

"Thank you, my friend." Black Hawk grinned. "Your soft bed is gentle on these old bones."

Reluctantly, Mac got up and prepared his pack for the long trip, knowing Black Hawk would not be there when he returned. *Into Your hands, Lord.*

For weapons he brought his Kentucky long rifle, his bow and arrows, and a knife he kept in the side of his boot. He packed a few pemmican cakes. He'd hunt on the trail and let Mrs. Danner barter for home-canned vegetables and fruit. He had to admit, her cooking on the open fire set with his stomach a lot better than the pemmican.

His throat thick, he embraced his old friend and left him with a final warning. "Be careful of Jasper. I expect he'll pay the cabin a visit."

"I may be old, but my ears still hear like a hawk." He winked.

"God bless you, my friend. I'll see you in glory."

Black Hawk's eyes watered. "I'll be there."

ช

Pamela appreciated the heart behind the words Calvin Turner had shared. Mary mentioned they had suffered losses similar to her own. She'd scream if one more person called Quinton her husband, but to tell them the truth would be to tell Mac the truth, and she couldn't trust him with that bit of information.

In some small way it made sense to let him believe the lie. She felt safe. A recently widowed woman would be treated with respect by a God-fearing man. And Mac gave all indication that he was a God-fearing man. Someone like Jasper she should fear. Would she be safe in Creelsboro, owning and operating a store? Would the men in town let her do it? Nothing made sense anymore. Nothing.

She rummaged through the wagon and finally found the chest she'd been looking for. The one with fine linens. Mary and her family could use these. It seemed the perfect gift. It was practical and yet also fancy—something to decorate their tables. From another chest she pulled out a bolt of thick cotton cloth. Perfect for making shirts, dresses, and even some light trousers for the hot summer months, not that they'd wear them for awhile.

Then the idea struck her to place the remaining linens in her trunk and her dresses and undergarments in the trunk with the money. Her task completed, she jumped down from the wagon, grabbed the items for the Turners, and headed for the house.

"Need a hand?" Mac strained a smile and stepped past her, placing a large pack in the back of the wagon.

"Oh, you're back." Pamela squelched her surprise. "Thank you. I'm giving these to Mary."

He nodded.

"Is something wrong?"

"Nothing." He took the two bundles from her arms and started toward the house. He stopped and turned back to look at her. "Anything else?"

"No." *Who are you, Mac? And what is so heavy on your heart?* Did he not want to take her to Creelsboro? Was he only doing it because of a promise to her brother? Should she hire someone else? *Perhaps Calvin. He could use some money with the new baby coming, couldn't he?*

"Thank you for asking them to bring Quinton's trunks down."

"You're welcome."

"I gave them to the Turners as well."

He raised an eyebrow.

"What? Should I have kept them?"

"No. You have no need for the items, and they can make use of some of them. It's practical."

"And by that you're implying that I'm not?"

He looked down at his feet.

"Look." She poked her finger into his chest. "I'll have you know I'm quite practical."

He glanced back at the wagon.

"What?"

He fumbled with the bolts of cloth. "Do you know how difficult it will be to take that wagon on the trail?"

"Some. But the trail's been used for years. It's a well-worn highway now."

Mac lowered his head but not fast enough. She saw his snicker.

"What are you telling me, or not telling me, as seems to be your way of communicating?"

He looked back at her, fire in his eyes. He opened his mouth, then promptly closed it. "Let's just say your concept of the trail has no basis in reality. You society folks always have a problem with that."

"Society folks? Oh, I get it. You think you're better than I am because you live off the land. You think that because I come from a place that has actual roads and rules, laws that are enforced, I have no logic? Let me tell you, you couldn't be farther from the truth. My logic works just fine. And when we arrive in Cumberland Ford, I'll find another who will take me to Creelsboro. Someone who doesn't feel so high and mighty about himself." She huffed and marched off to the house.

Just who does he think he is, telling me who I am and not knowing the first thing about me? I'll admit I picked the wrong traveling shoes. . . . But Quinton had led her to believe the road was like the streets in Virginia. Perhaps not cobblestone, but the ground would have been well trod and hardened from the many, many people traveling along it for the past fifty-seven years or so.

A high-pitched whistle whizzed past her ear. Mac grabbed her by the waist and pushed her to the ground. Wood splintered from the log siding of the house.

six

"Stay down," Mac whispered. The shot had come from the foothills.

Will pulled open the front door, squatted down, and ran over to them. "Who was that? Jasper?"

"I don't know. Take Mrs. Danner inside. I'll find out."

"I'll be right behind you," Will informed him. "Not all of the children are in the house."

"I'll keep an eye out." Mac released the frightened woman. He had to admit she had spunk.

Mac crawled on his belly toward the barn. He didn't plan on beating Black Hawk to heaven. He worked a wide circle from behind the barn up to the edge of the trees. The shooter couldn't have gotten too far. He hadn't heard any rustle in the underbrush. Birds were beginning to sing again. Obviously, the person was lying low.

He turned and saw Will working his way around the barn. Hopefully, the children were playing in there.

Stealthily, he worked his way through the underbrush, careful not to make a sound. A mumbled whimpering caught his ears. He turned toward the southeast. *Crying? Someone was crying?*

"Hello," he called out.

The sobs increased. Mac picked up his pace. The voice of a young one. *Dear God, please let them be safe.*

He broke through the underbrush and came upon Jason, with a pistol lying at his feet. "Jason, are you all right?"

The large brown eyes stared back at him. Black smudges

ran from side to side across his cheeks.

"Target practice?" Mac asked.

The boy nodded his head. Mac opened his arms, and he came running into them. "I didn't mean to shoot her. Is she alive?"

"You missed, thank the Lord. What were you aiming at?"

The child pointed to a tree about ninety degrees away from the house.

"I'm not your pa, but I think you're a bit too young to be shooting."

"Jason?" Will shouted, gasping for air.

"I'm sorry, Grandpa. I didn't mean to."

Will simply embraced the child and headed with him back to the house. Mac picked up the pistol, checked the barrel, and found it warped. *No wonder he hit the house.*

He heard Will send out a familiar whistle, a sound that let everyone know all was well. Soon, folks started coming out of the house. Mac felt certain Calvin would be taking Jason out behind the barn later. *But I think Jason will find that a welcome relief.* The fear of what might have happened in that boy's eyes sent a chill down his own spine.

One person hadn't emerged from the Turner home. Mrs. Danner. How had he gotten on the wrong foot with her two minutes after he returned? *And Black Hawk thinks I ought to marry her? He has no idea what this woman is really like. She's so self-consumed.*

Mac gnawed his inner cheek, reassessing that judgment. *She did willingly give the trunks to Will and his family.*

Mac took in a deep breath and let it out slowly. *Guess I need to go see if the widow is all right.* After a few minutes greeting the various members of the family, he entered the house. The living area was empty. The kitchen, too. *Where is she?* Then he saw her exit the room she'd slept in with a small carpetbag in tow. "And just where do you think you're going?"

"Cumberland Ford. There's a tavern I can stay at." She walked past him as if he weren't there.

"No, you're not." He reached out and grabbed her elbow.

She glared at his hand. Hot daggers of emotion singed his heart. He released his grasp.

&

"I absolve you of my, my. . .of Quinton's dying wish." *Why can't I tell him he's my brother?* Pamela wondered. *What am I afraid of?*

"Absolve all you want, Mrs. Danner, but that doesn't change that I'm a man of my word." His voice remained tight but controlled.

Pamela shivered at the thought of this mountain of a man ever losing control.

"Mrs. Danner, perhaps we've gotten off on the wrong foot here. I wish to honor Mr. Danner's request to take you to Creelsboro. And I will try to not make judgments about your social upbringing. Truce?"

Pamela relaxed her shoulders. "I appreciate your concern, Mr. MacKenneth, but I think it best if I should try and find another traveling companion. You and I tend to be fire and ice."

"More like fire and gunpowder," he mumbled.

Pamela chuckled. "You may be right there. Seriously, though, I've been giving this a lot of thought, and I've concluded I should ask Calvin or one of the others to take me."

"Calvin, with his child due soon? You can't be serious."

"Yes, you're right. He'd need to stay by his wife. Perhaps one of the other brothers. I'm sure they could use the money."

"At the moment I think they're all rather busy discussing firearms and safety with all their children."

"Oh dear, I heard it was safe. What happened? I just assumed it was a stray bullet."

"Jason was target practicing without permission. Calvin will be quite busy with the boy for awhile."

Pamela resisted the urge to rub her backside. On more than one occasion, she'd been the recipient of such instruction. Thankfully, her infractions had never revolved around a firearm.

"Mrs. Danner, I am the most logical choice to take you west. I have no family obligations, and I have no business that would need my attention."

"What do you do?"

"I'm a fur trader. But as I mentioned to you before, during the spring and summer I'm a farmer."

Pam sat down on a wooden chair. Handmade, she presumed. "I don't know, Mr. MacKenneth. The trip will be long and hard. I have enough grief dealing with Quinton's death, the loss of my parents, and. . ." She shook her head. He wouldn't understand how others had made plans on her behalf. A man like Mac lived his own life.

☙

Why am I fighting with her to continue the trip? She's right. She could find someone else. Even one of the Turner brothers would do a great job. Why am I insisting? Mac turned and walked over to the one window in the front of the log cabin.

There had been no further evidence that Jasper would pursue them. Even Black Hawk wouldn't fault him for letting the woman go with whomever she felt more comfortable. He pulled off his coonskin cap and wiped his brow.

He glanced back at the young widow. Fine yellow hair concealed Mrs. Danner's face, her head bent as if in prayer. Her fingers knit together. Water-filled blue orbs appeared and stared back at him.

"Mr. MacKenneth. . ."

"Mac," he corrected.

"Mac," she continued. "You'll probably think less of me than you do already, but you seem to be a bad omen. Every time you appear, something bad happens. And personally, I've faced enough hardships. I don't want to risk more."

Mac mentally picked his jaw up from the floor, clamping his mouth shut so he wouldn't speak a word out of turn.

"Quinton died shortly after you arrived. Jasper showed up on the trail; and since you've returned, I've been shot at. Don't you think that's more than coincidence?"

Lord, give me the right words here. I don't want to alienate this woman further. "There is another side to what you've presented."

"What's that?" Her eyes searched his as if longing to be proven wrong.

Slowly he made his way over to her as if approaching a fawn. "God may have had me there to help you just when you needed it."

She blinked.

"How would you have removed that wagon from Quinton?" He paused, letting the question penetrate. "How would you have dealt with Jasper if you had managed to get Quinton free and had continued on the road?"

A tear trickled down her right cheek. He raised a finger to remove it, then thought better. Scanning the room, he lowered his voice. "And if I hadn't been here, you might have been hit by Jason's bullet."

She opened her mouth a fraction to speak. For the first time, he noticed how perfect her lips were, the perfect shade of pink for her fair complexion, carefully riding the contours of her mouth. *Whoa!* Mac jumped up and retreated to the window. He kept his back toward her, his stance rigid. Where had those thoughts come from? It was all Black Hawk's fault. *If only he hadn't suggested I need a wife.* Who was he fooling?

The woman was beautiful. He'd never seen anyone finer. He had to protect her. Glancing over his shoulder, he wondered how much he'd have to protect her from himself.

A knock at the doorway broke his wayward thoughts.

"Is it safe to come in now?" Mary smiled.

Mac felt the heat rise on the back of his neck. If he'd been wearing a four-in-hand, he'd be pulling at the collar of his shirt.

"Beggin' your pardon, Pamela, but you're a different woman around Mac. And, Mac, I've never seen you raise your voice at anyone before. To see you've done that to a widow. . . You should be ashamed of yourself." Mary put on her white linen apron and went straight to the kitchen.

They had been heard arguing. *Great.* He winced. "I apologize, Mary. I'll be in the barn if you change your mind, Mrs. Danner." He slipped on his cap and hiked over to the barn.

He examined the wagon. Why had he lost his temper with Mrs. Danner? What had caused them to blow up with each other in the first place? He tried to think back. Nothing. Then his words, "It's practical," echoed through his mind. Mac leaned against the wagon and let his head bang against it. He was no good with women. Never had been. Why was he the one being dragged across the country with her? Surely God could have found a better man.

And perhaps that was the real problem. He was fighting God's choices for his life. Mac squeezed his eyes shut and rubbed his forehead with his thumb and first finger. *Why did You lead me down that road, Lord, at that particular time?* The answer that he was needed was too easy. Perhaps there was more to Mrs. Danner's situation than simply needing a guide to Creelsboro. Perhaps God had chosen to use this opportunity to teach Mac to trust Him on a new level.

Mac slid to the ground and sat with his knees to his chest. He'd always considered himself a Good Samaritan of sorts, willing to go the extra mile for others. Of course, his lifestyle limited the contact he had with others. He gnawed his lower lip.

"Heard ya hollerin' at Pamela Danner. What's that all about?" Will Jr. asked as he came in and towered over him.

"I've just been trying to figure it out myself."

Will Jr. tossed back his head and laughed. "Ya don't figure out women, my friend, ya only figure out how to live with them."

"I don't need to figure that out. I'm not *living* with her."

"You most certainly are if you're taking her halfway across the state." Will Jr. sat down beside him. "Tell me, what's the real problem ya have with her?"

"She's unbelievably impractical. Just look at the contents of this wagon. I can't imagine how we're going to get this across the river."

"Several trips?" Will Jr. quipped.

"That's the problem. A trip that would take maybe five days at a good run could take two weeks, perhaps more."

"I see. You think she should just run across the state like you?" Will Jr. narrowed his gaze, his bushy brown eyebrows knit together. "No one runs like you. I swear you're half Indian."

Mac was tempted to tell Will that Black Hawk was back in the area but decided against it. The fewer who knew, the safer his old friend would be. "I admit I'd rather run than ride."

"That's what I'm saying. You're more comfortable with that. Me, I prefer a horse. I get there quickly, and I'm not hot and sweaty."

Mac chuckled and nodded his head. "No, I'm not expecting the woman to run across the state. But couldn't she lighten the load some?"

"Aren't the contents of this wagon what she needs to run her business in Creelsboro?"

"I reckon. I think they would have been wise to ship it through a northern route or have it delivered shortly after they arrived."

"I see. Now you're a man who knows how to run a store."

"Don't go twisting my words, Will. I made no such boast. I'm just speaking logic, pure and simple logic."

"To you, yes. But what about the rest of us who don't live the way you do? I, for one, am pleased to have some of her husband's wares. I ain't seen much and, well, it's nice to get dressed up for the missus every once and again."

"I wouldn't know," Mac mumbled.

Will Jr. placed his hand on Mac's shoulder. "She's gone, Mac. Leave her in God's hands and stop thinking every woman is the same as Tilly."

"I should have known better. It's my fault."

"We've been over this ground before, my friend, and you know my feelings on the matter. I've said my piece. I'll leave ya to your thoughts."

Mac molded his beard with his hand. Had he been reacting as if Mrs. Danner were Tilly?

☙

Pamela looked down at the carpetbag on her lap. Heat rose on her cheeks. The entire Turner clan had heard them arguing. Pamela closed her eyes and tried to focus. Taking in a deep breath, she stood and walked into the kitchen area. "Mary, I'm sorry for my outburst."

Mary turned and motioned for her to sit down. Pam did.

"Pamela, what are you afraid of with Mac? He's a good and decent man. Generally he keeps to himself, but I've never heard a complaint from anyone. What did he do to you?"

"Nothing. . .everything. . .I don't know. From the moment we met, he's been telling me what to do and how poorly I've been doing everything else. I'd be the first to admit I made a poor selection in my shoes, but that does not give him the right to think of me as addlepated with no thoughts or feelings for anyone but myself."

"Ah." Mary poured two cups of tea.

"One minute he seems like the kindest and gentlest man I've ever known; the next he's carrying on like a bear denied his favorite honey tree."

Mary chuckled.

"What?"

"You're taken with him, aren't you?"

"No." Pamela, realizing her voice had risen, lowered it. "I mean, he's not a bad-looking man in a huge, bear kind of way, I reckon, but. . ."

"Quinton wasn't your husband, was he?"

Pamela buried her hands in her face. "No, he was my brother. How did you know?"

"No ring, Dear. And you've not referred to him once as your husband. You're grieving, that's clear. But after Calvin spoke with you, I was certain of it." Mary reached over and placed her hand on Pamela's.

"Mac assumed we were married. I've simply not corrected the error. I figure I'm safer being single and alone with a stranger if he thinks I'm a new widow. And I do ache."

Mary sipped her tea. "This area is wilderness. Your life can be placed in danger very easily, and Mac is a man of his word. If he promised your brother that he'd take you to Creelsboro, then that is what he'll do. He'll probably continue to be hard on the realities of wilderness living. He, more than most others, knows what he's talkin' 'bout."

"What do you mean?" Pamela held the cup in her hand.

"That's for him to say, if the time is right. Just as you have your own secret. I wager the good Lord is none too pleased with you stretching the truth."

Thankfully, Mary hadn't called her a liar. Pam didn't need someone to spell it out. She sipped her tea to keep from justifying her actions. What could she say? She shouldn't let Mac believe the lie. On the other hand, he was just as guilty in letting Jasper believe she was Mac's wife. No, it was better that he be left with his misimpressions.

"You're welcome to spend the night here," Mary added. "It's late and will be dark before you reach Cumberland Ford. I wouldn't want you running into Jasper or any other bandit along the way."

Pamela rubbed her arms. For some reason she'd been hoping Jasper had moved on. "If he's that bad of a man, why don't you have him arrested?"

"Can't prove he's done anything." Mary rose from the table. "No one's survived. No one's seen him actually commit a crime. And the local law is in Barbourville. Cumberland Ford might be getting someone soon. Hard to say. Lawmen and preachers are in short supply in these parts. Folks don't plan long engagements. Once they hear a preacher is coming, they line up. Though that's been changing some with the one at the Ford settlement all the time."

Preachers and lawmen. Weren't they the cornerstone of a healthy community? How can people live like this, Lord? No law, no order? "Thanks for the tea. I'll speak with Mr. MacKenneth and see if he'd prefer to spend the night or not."

"Fair enough. Dinner will be ready shortly."

The scent of a hearty stew passed Pamela's nostrils. How could she have missed its fine aroma? *Because your mind was on something else,* she reprimanded herself.

She found Mac sitting on the barn floor, leaning against a wagon wheel. "Mac?"

He opened his eyes and turned to look at her. "I'm sorry," he apologized.

"I'm sorry, too. You're right. I don't know what came over me. You are the best choice to take me to Creelsboro."

He nodded.

"Mary would like to know if we'd like to leave tonight or wait until morning."

"If you're agreeable, tonight is fine. If we leave right away. However, if we wait another thirty minutes, it'd be best to wait until morning."

"Now is fine. It's hard to face everyone after having made such a fool of myself."

"We're both in that place, I reckon. Let's say our good-byes and be off then."

"Fine." She tossed her carpetbag in the front of the wagon. It had been a pleasant visit with the Turners, but it was time to move on.

A black cat scurried past her. Pamela froze.

seven

"What's the matter?" Mac scanned the area, looking for danger.

"I think we should wait until tomorrow." She reached back to the wagon and grabbed her carpetbag.

"What's the matter?" He fought down his temper. What had she seen or heard to scare her? Wouldn't he have heard any real danger?

She stood resolute, shaking her head slightly.

He stepped up to her and placed his hands on her shoulders. "Mrs. Danner, Pamela, you need to trust me. Tell me what has frightened you."

Fresh tears filled her eyes. "You wouldn't understand."

"Try me." He brushed a wayward strand of gold from her eyes.

"I'd been warned before we left that this trip would be disastrous. And it has been that. Now that I've determined to go on to Creelsboro, the very next thing that happens is. . ." She broke her gaze and looked at the straw-covered floor. "You'll just think me foolish."

He placed his forefinger under her chin, prompting her to look at him. A strong desire to protect her coursed through his veins. "Trust me," he whispered.

"I know you'll think this is idle foolishness, but a black cat just crossed my path. It's another omen, a warning. I don't think we should leave tonight."

If it hadn't been for how frightened she'd become, he would have roared with laughter. No one should ever be frightened by Blacky. That animal barely caught the mice he was supposed to catch. Blacky was more skittish than any creature Mac had ever seen. He found it amazing Pamela had even seen the animal.

"I don't believe in omens. I believe God is stronger than anything we'll face and will protect us. However, if you'd prefer to wait 'til morning, we shall wait."

"Thank you." She sighed. "I'm sorry. I know most people find these things nonsense."

"Like I said, I don't believe in 'em, but I know folks who do."

He watched as calmness played across the tranquil blue of her eyes. A desire to wrap her in his arms and pull her toward him startled him. He released his hold of her shoulders. Heat rose on the back of his neck. There were blessings to having long hair, he mused.

"I'll let Mary know to expect two more for dinner." She slipped past him.

"Sounds good. I'll see if I can hunt down a wild turkey to help replenish what we've eaten."

Pamela paused and turned back toward him. "Oh my, I hadn't thought of that. I have some canned goods in the wagon. Should I fetch a couple items?"

"I've never seen a woman can or prepare more food than Mary. But they have a large family. What do you have that they might not?" Mac inquired.

"Sugar, what about sugar? Don't folks out here run low on that?" Pamela climbed up into the wagon and started to move crates.

"Tend to. I'm sure Mary would appreciate such a generous gift, but. . ." Mac rubbed the back of his neck. "Will Jr. said you've given them a lot already. They might be offended, with them just being neighborly and all. It's a fine line. I, on the other hand, haven't contributed anything."

Pamela sat down on a crate. "I don't want to give too much. Quinton always said I was too generous. He's the business-man, not me."

How would this woman survive running her husband's business? Would she give it all away? Would she know when to order, to restock? Did she understand what kinds of sup-plies were needed for folks heading west? *Lord, give this woman direction.* "I think you've given enough. Let me help you down from there."

"Do you think I can find a new pair of shoes in Cumberland Ford?"

"Not likely. Closest place would be Barbourville, but that's three days down the road."

She nodded. "We'll plan on buying me a pair of rugged boots then."

Maybe he had misjudged her. She definitely had problems with her faith, mixing it up with omens. But perhaps she wasn't as impractical as he'd first suspected. He helped her down and grabbed his cap. "Go tell Mary we're spending another night. I'll be back in an hour."

Mac set a quick pace and ran into the woods at the bottom of the mountain. Wild turkeys were plentiful in these hills and something he knew the Turner family enjoyed. He stopped and scanned the ground for tracks. Turkey tracks could be easily missed in this terrain, but Black Hawk had trained him well. There, he spotted some. He worked his way deeper into the woods and placed an arrow on his bow. He spotted a flock and took aim. The gentle twang of the bowstring sent the arrow flying, hitting its mark. The remaining birds scattered as he picked up the gift and headed back.

The smell of a campfire caught his attention. He circled around and found it. The fire had been hastily put out, the camp abandoned. He looked around. Three men, possibly four, had spent a fair amount of time in this spot. Mac put more dirt on the dying embers and continued back to the Turners. Had Jasper given up his watch?

ʑ

The next morning, Pam and Mac headed north toward the Cumberland Ford camp. They talked little. She'd been worrying all night if she'd made the right decision to continue the trip to Creelsboro. Her heart wasn't in running a business, certainly not in a community where no one stayed for long. From what she recalled her father saying about Creelsboro, it was one of the last stops for people heading west. Day in and day out, people arrived, spent a day or two, and left. It also occurred to her that a riverfront town probably had lots of taverns selling spirits. The prospect of being a woman alone in that kind of environment didn't excite her.

An hour into the trip she began to relax. The mountains seemed so peaceful. The winter branches seemed less threatening somehow. She imagined what they would be like in the spring when the trees bloomed.

"We're almost there," Mac said.

"We cross the Cumberland here, correct?"

"Yes, Ma'am. We'll cross the river near the ford and try to avoid the toll. We'll see how high the water is. This time of year, it shouldn't be too bad. The wagon is heavy. We might have to unload and carry some items across, then bring the wagon over."

Like when Quinton had to get the wagon across the gap. Her heart beat wildly. She stared straight ahead. Her hands clasped the bench seat of the wagon. "Pay the toll, cross at the ford," she ordered.

"What's wrong?" he asked.

"Nothing," she demurred.

He pulled back slightly on the reins, slowing down the pace

of the horses. "Your knuckles are white. What's wrong?"

"I just thought of Quinton and. . .and the accident."

"I'm sorry. We'll cross at the ford."

"I've noticed you use rather strange terms." She needed to get her mind off Quinton and the accident as it replayed over and over again in her mind. "Like 'flank,' but you weren't talking about the flank of a horse. You were referring to the mountain."

"Has the same meaning—*side of*. The houses flanked the north side of the mountain."

"Do folks heading west carry pemmican?"

"I can't say. I picked it up from my Indian friend Black Hawk."

Pamela's eyebrows rose. "I thought the Indians were gone. They still live here?"

"No, they've been moved to the reservation in Indian Territory. It's hard to have peace about our need for land and expansion while seeing the Indians moved out. I think it would have been better if we could have embraced them, learned from them, learned how to live with them. But our ways are very different from their ways. I don't have an answer for what's right. But somehow it doesn't seem fair that a group of people who have lived for many generations in an area have to be sent out to live somewhere else."

Pamela hadn't given the issue much thought. She'd only heard the stories of how the Indians had killed so many white people. She feared them, as many of her friends did. And yet this man beside her had befriended an Indian, perhaps more than one. If nothing else, this trip was teaching her about different people and their ways.

They spent the night at the Renfroes', finding the Colsons' tavern, where Mac had stayed during other journeys, already full. The next morning they traversed the ford. The river was quite low, and they crossed easily. Pamela paid a toll of sixty-three cents. "Highway robbery," Mac muttered.

"I hope to get us up to Flatlick by nightfall," Mac offered as they resumed their perch on the wagon's bench.

"What's in Flatlick?"

"Not much. It's one of the oldest settlements in the state. The horses will love it there—still plenty of salt for them to lick. Years ago hunters found it an easy way to hunt bison. The animals would come up to the lick, and the hunters would pick them off from behind the bushes."

Pamela scrunched up her nose. "Doesn't seem fair to the animal."

Mac chuckled. "When providing for your family's needs, fair doesn't come into play. A man can go out and run the countryside hunting down his dinner, or he can wait where he knows the animal will come to him. There really isn't much choice."

"But you don't hunt that way."

"No, but I follow the animals' trails and find the right place to attack."

"Why do you trap animals for their fur?"

"Because it's a job I can do in the wilderness that provides for my needs."

"What needs do you have?" Pam wasn't trying to be insulting, but she really couldn't imagine this man needing much of anything. His clothing was made from animal skins; his hat from a raccoon; his boots, leather. His rifle was manmade, but he used a bow and arrow, too.

Mac chuckled. "Not many. I tend to put the money into the family farm. Someday I'll have to settle down and take care of it. But for now, my parents manage just fine."

"Why the wilderness?"

"I don't know. I suppose it's because it's wide open and lets me be alone most of the time. I kinda like it that way."

"Oh." She'd talked too much, she supposed. She'd been told more than once by her brother to just stop talking. She'd found it especially hard on him as they traveled. When they were alone, the only person to talk with was Quinton. Now, Mac was there, and she'd started talking with him as easily as she had with her brother. "Do you suppose Jasper is still following us?"

"Haven't seen a sign of him since the night before we left the Turners'. I'm starting to think he's gone on."

Pamela breathed a sigh of relief. The constant threat of a bandit around the corner had started to weigh on her nerves. Finally she could relax.

❧

Mac scanned the skies. A large ridge of dark clouds was heading their way. "Pamela, we need to move quickly. That storm is coming in fast."

"Tell me what to do." Her eyes blazed with excitement.

"Hang on. I'm going to try to beat this storm." He slapped the reins. "Yah!"

The horses bolted forward. Mac kept a firm grasp of the reins. The rough trail, rutted from the herds of cattle using the road, made the wagon buck and bounce. He glanced at Pamela. She held on tight without complaining. Could he have misjudged her?

They were a mile out from Flatlick when the first bits of sleet hit.

"Ow!" she cried out.

"Cover your face."

The horses were breathing heavily. He slowed down the pace.

"I'm cold. How bad is this storm going to be?"

"It'll be a rough one. We'll find a place to stay, and I'll take care of the horses. They'll need a good rubdown and a treat. Got any more of those apples?" He smiled.

"For you or the horses?"

"Both." He broadened his grin.

There was little question he enjoyed traveling with a cook. Every place they stopped, Pamela would barter or pay for fresh vegetables and eggs. He'd been eating better on the road than he had been in his own cabin. He'd forgotten how much he loved vegetables with his meals. Summers on the farm, he always had healthy helpings of meat, biscuits, and vegetables to round out his meals. During winters in his cabin, however, that luxury disappeared. He kept plenty of fresh meat around. But because he needed to travel light on his way to the cabin, the extra weight of canned vegetables or even root vegetables had proved prohibitive. Perhaps he could look into planting something in the early spring that would still be there when he returned in the fall.

The wind howled.

"How. . .much. . .longer, Mac?" She shivered.

"Almost there. See that curl of smoke?"

"No, but I trust you."

Mac grinned. They were becoming more comfortable with each other as the trip wore on.

He pulled onto one of the many side trails he'd seen along the road. It amazed him how fast this area was growing each year. There were more trails to other farmers' homes. The Campbells had been in this area longer than most. They'd open their home, Mac knew, especially for a woman.

Their farmhouse came into view on the left. It was framed by a long, front pasture with fields on the left and right. A smaller plain filled the space between the back of the house and the side of the mountain.

"Whoa." He pulled the wagon to a stop. "I'll be right back."

He raised his hand to knock on the front door, but an older man in his fifties opened it first. Mac extended his hand. "Art

Campbell, Nash MacKenneth. Folks call me Mac. I heard you put folks up from time to time."

"Ain't got no more room. Storm's threatening to be a bad one. There's room in the barn, if you don't mind sleeping there. It even has an old woodstove. But you be careful, now. Make sure there's nothing that can catch fire."

"Thank you." Mac pumped his hand.

"You and your missus take care now." Art slipped back into the house and shut the door.

A few quick strides and Mac was back by the side of the wagon. "There's no room in the house, but there's room in the barn. Do you mind?"

"Do I mind? Anything is better than this." Pamela held a woolen blanket close to her chest.

"All right then, let's go make that barn our home for the night or until this storm passes." He snapped the reins. "Yah."

They entered the protection of the barn within a couple minutes. "Stay there and warm up," he directed. "I'll take care of the horses."

"No." Her teeth chattered. "I think I need to move to get my blood flowing."

"All right. Mr. Campbell said there was an old woodstove in here somewhere." Mac scanned the barn for a chimney. "Over there. Make sure there's nothing around to catch fire, and I'll get us a fire started in a minute."

She nodded, and he went to work unbuckling the horses. The stalls were filled with other peoples' horses and mules. A milk cow lowed in a rear corner. He eyed a hayloft where he'd be able to fashion a bed for them. Mac shook his head. Correction, two beds for them. He'd done well to keep his growing desires to himself. *Father, give me strength. She's a widow, and You know I'm lousy with women.*

"Mac!" Pamela screamed.

eight

Pamela dropped to her hands and knees. The end of a shotgun was not what she'd planned on seeing.

"What?" Mac came running.

The barrel slipped back out through a hole in the wall. "A barrel from a gun was pointing in at us."

"Where?" Mac frantically searched the barn.

"Through that hole." She pointed to the large knothole in the barn board.

He knelt down.

"Careful."

He waved for her to stay down, as if she were going to stand up and give someone an easy target. He looked through the crack between the wooden planks before peering out the hole. "You scared 'em off, whoever it was."

"Or they moved to another side of the barn."

"I'll go check. Do you know how to shoot?"

She shook her head no.

"Great," he mumbled. "Why didn't I try and teach you before now?"

He went to the wagon, pulled out his Kentucky long rifle, loaded, and cocked it. "Here, keep it pointed at the door. All you have to do is pull the trigger. I'll holler before I open it. Please, try not to shoot me."

She was tempted to say something coy but thought it better to hold her tongue. Mac's sense of humor wasn't the same as her own. He lined the gun up and set the barrel resting on the wagon, aimed toward the doors.

He slipped through the doors, not making a sound. *How's he do that?* she wondered. Several times over the past couple days she'd seen him walk as if he were a feather, barely leaving an impression on the ground and never making a sound.

A huge thud against the side of the barn startled Pamela. Her focus shifted away from the barn door to the wall where she heard the noise. Realizing her error, she went back to her sentry post.

"I'm coming in, Pamela," Mac hollered. She lifted her head from the line of sight on the rifle barrel. Beside Mac stood a skinny, redheaded youngster with tattered clothing. "This here is Urias. He apparently has been sleeping in Art Campbell's barn for awhile."

"And I take it Mr. Campbell is unaware."

A sly grin slid up the boy's face. He placed his hands in his pockets and shrugged his shoulders.

"Hungry?" Pamela asked. She wasn't about to tattle on the boy during the storm. After the storm might be another matter.

"I'll light the fire." Mac encouraged the boy into the room with a slight nudge forward. He uncocked his rifle and placed it back in the wagon. Lifting the canvas over the rear of the wagon, he grabbed some wood.

Pamela removed a Dutch oven, a knife, cutting board, some vegetables, water, and the biscuits she'd made earlier in the morning. "Mac, what meat would you like me to use? There's some ham, bacon, or your pemmican. I'm thinking a hearty stew would be in order tonight."

"Ham or pemmican is fine with me. Let's have the bacon and eggs in the morning. You're up for bacon and eggs, aren't you, Urias? Come and give me a hand with the horses."

Urias did as he was told but didn't speak a word. How Mac had gotten any information out of the boy before they came back to the barn was beyond her comprehension.

Pam went to work making a stew for the three of them. She also pulled a thick cotton blanket out of the wagon to use as a tablecloth to cover the dust and straw of the barn. She'd have to go into the crates to find another plate, silverware, and cup for Urias. The boy probably hadn't eaten well in a long time.

The casket of water was full. She could sponge bathe later. If she could find a private spot, she mused. Looking around the barn, she felt grateful it provided shelter, but they'd have to be well covered for the entire night. The stove was small, too small for the size of the barn. It wouldn't heat all night. But it would help some, and at least it gave them a place to cook a warm meal.

"Pam, Urias and I need to clean up. Did you warm some water on the stove?" Mac grinned. He'd never asked for warm water to clean up with before. He'd always just gone to the river. The boy was walking comfortably around Mac now.

"Yes. Dinner's ready whenever you two are," Pamela called out to them.

"Be right there."

Pamela heard some whispering. *Urias was talking?*

She served up the three plates of the thick stew, along with one biscuit each.

Mac paused to say a prayer. "Father, we thank Thee for this barn. We thank Thee for this warm food for our bellies, and we ask Thee for protection from the storm. In Jesus' name. Amen."

"Amen." Pamela raised her bowed head.

"Amen," Urias mumbled.

Pamela jumped up. "I almost forgot. I purchased a treat at the Cumberland Ford settlement. Mrs. Renfro was so sweet," she continued as she hiked back to the wagon. Fumbling through the small area in the rear where she kept her kitchen, she found the small jar of peach preserves. She had planned to save it for a special time, but now seemed as good a time as any.

"Peach preserves on biscuits." Mac licked his lips. "Woman, you know how to please a hungry man." Their eyes locked. Pamela shivered from the connection she felt. *How can this be?*

‪&‪

"Wonderful meal, Pamela, really hit the spot," Mac complimented. "What did you think, Urias?"

"It's good, thanks."

The boy had gobbled the food down like he hadn't eaten in a week, *which he probably hasn't,* Mac guessed.

"Is there more?" Urias held out his empty plate.

Pamela took it. "Of course there is." She went to the stove and promptly filled his plate to the brim again. "I'm afraid there aren't any more biscuits, but I'll be making some later."

"Thanks, they're wonderful. You cook good." He smacked his lips and dove his fork into the mound of food. Mac glanced over at Pamela and winked. What had happened between them earlier still warmed his heart—and terrified him.

"Urias, after you're done, you can help me set up the loft for sleeping."

"Sure," he said with his mouth full. "I usually sleep over there." He pointed to a stall now holding one of the house occupant's mules. "There's a loose board that moves enough so I can wiggle into the barn."

Mac wanted to know more of why the boy was on the run, but he needed to win his trust first. He appeared to be around fourteen, maybe a young fifteen.

"Pamela, I'll fix you a bed with sheets and blankets if you have some linens for me."

"Let me get them. How cold do you think it will get tonight?"

"It's freezing now, and the sun just set. I'd say it'll drop another ten to fifteen degrees."

"I don't have three wool blankets," she stammered. "I have another thick cotton one like the one I put down on the floor over there," she offered. "We could set the tent up and that might give us some additional warmth."

"The various blankets should do nicely. I'll even show you a trick later. You'll be warmer than you've ever been by the time I get through with you."

Pamela flushed.

"I–I mean by preparing a special bed for you." Mac's throat thickened. *How could I have implied something so forward?* He hadn't meant it the way it sounded. He knew his motives were pure. Mac groaned and headed toward the loft. He'd only planned to lay a healthy layer of hay over her once she was down for the night. How could planning to do something nice for the woman have gotten so garbled in the offering?

Urias joined him a few minutes later with bundles of blankets. "How much stuff do you have packed in that wagon?"

"You don't want to know." Mac closed his eyes at the thought. She'd pulled out something new just about once a day. She had more items stuffed in places he couldn't imagine. He'd wondered that first day why the wagon sat so low. Now he knew. She utilized every bit of space to the fullest.

"What do you need me to do?" Urias offered.

"I'm trying to make a comfortable place for Pamela. I don't want a draft to come up from under her, but I don't want the hay too hard. I'm fashioning some walls here to help hold her body heat in a closer area."

"Where'd you learn all this?"

"I grew up on a farm."

"You don't look like a farmer." Urias started molding the hay.

Mac continued working the hay, trying to catch glimpses of the boy every now and again, hoping to gain a better understanding of him. "During the winters I'm a fur trapper. What about you? What are you doing?"

"Can't find a job. Wrong time of the year."

"Where'd you get the rifle?"

"It's mine." He instantly stood, his body rigid.

"I'm not saying it isn't. I'm just asking. Where'd you come by it?" It was more than likely the one item Urias had taken from his home when he decided to run.

The boy's shoulders relaxed and he went back to work. "My pa gave it to me when I was ten."

"Not a bad rifle. Needs a good oiling. Did your pa teach you how to do that?"

"He never got the chance." Urias's eyes watered.

"I'll be happy to show you. I've got to take care of mine."

A smile as wide as the gap spread across the boy's freckled face. "Really? Thanks."

"You're more than welcome. Come on, let's go shape our bed."

"Our bed? Aren't you sleeping with your wife?"

"No. Pamela will sleep better without me." If Urias only knew. "I'm going to be up and down all night adding wood to the fire. Plus, once I put her in that hay cocoon, she won't want to get out."

"I'll have to remember that cocoon."

"Works really well, even in the wild when you only have pine needles around. You take a tarp of canvas, fold it in half, put a bed of needles under you, then pile the needles as high as you can find them around you and on top. I've often built a temporary shelter out of pine needles and branches."

"When did you start living in the wilderness?"

The boy's getting more comfortable with me. Thank You, Lord. "A few years older than you. I was eighteen."

"I'll be eighteen next year."

Mac scrutinized him, giving him the eye that said, *I know you're not being honest with me.*

Urias looked down at his feet. "Maybe in four years."

Mac smiled. Urias did the same. "Can you teach me how to make leather clothes like you have?"

"Not in one night but maybe in the future."

Urias placed his hands in his pockets. "I don't know how to survive out here."

Mac sat down in the hay and patted it for Urias to join him. "Why are you out here, Son?"

&

Pam made a batch of biscuits, prepared a loaf of bread to cook up in the morning, cleaned up, and still Mac and Urias hadn't come down. She even set some beans soaking, reasoning it might be late in the day tomorrow before they could travel on. Once, she'd gone over to listen and heard them talking about Urias living alone in the wilderness.

The wind whistled through the barn boards. Pamela stretched her back. She needed to get some sleep. "Mac," she called up at the base of the ladder to the loft.

"Sorry, Pamela, we were chewing the fat. Come on up. The bed is all ready for you."

Pamela started to climb up the flimsy ladder. "It's mighty dark up here."

"Shh, nothing to be afraid of. We won't be lighting a candle or a lamp with this much hay lying around." He winked and wrapped his arm around her waist, whispering in her ear, "Urias thinks we're married. I think it's better that way for now."

"All right." She trembled from his touch.

In full voice he said, "We have something special planned for you. Urias and I are going to sleep in this section."

"What are you planning on doing to me?" She let out a nervous laugh.

"Trust me."

"You'll like it, Mrs. Mac. I wouldn't mind if he did it to me."

Mac turned to him. "I can. Would you really like me to do it for you, Urias?"

"Yeah!" The boy's voice deepened, sounding more grown-up, less eager. Mac turned his back and held down a chuckle.

"First we get to show Pamela."

Pamela giggled. It couldn't be too bad if Urias would like it.

"Lie down here and make yourself comfortable," Mac instructed.

She lay down. "Oh, Mac, this is perfect."

"Not yet. Cover up."

She obeyed. The hay was soft and comfortable. The warmth of her body soon heated up the cool air surrounding her.

Mac tossed a pile of hay on top of her.

"Hey, what are you doing?" she protested.

"Trust me. I'm creating another layer of warmth. The hay will help your body stay warmer. You're not going to feel the drop in temperature at all tonight. Except possibly on your nose."

Pamela giggled, and Urias dumped another armful of hay upon her. Soon a mound of hay a foot tall covered her. She had freedom of movement, but the weight added the feel of a very thick quilt on top of her blanket.

"Good night, Pamela."

"Night, Mac."

Urias peeked over the mound of hay. "Does it feel good, Mrs. Mac?"

"Yes, very. Good night, Urias."

"Good night. Can you do me now, Mr. Mac?"

Pamela held back another laugh. The child was living in a grown-up world but still needed to be a child. She snuggled deeper in her soft bed. Who didn't need to be pampered like a child every now and again?

Urias giggled and gave a running commentary of Mac's

actions. They had bonded. *Lord, You know what Urias needs. I'm glad Mac was here to befriend the child. Perhaps he can help him find a new home. He has so many friends and acquaintances in the area, Lord. Surely someone would be willing to take him in.*

Pam closed her eyes and drifted off to sleep. The cares of this world, the storm, Jasper—they all left her. Mac was here. She was safe.

❧

Pamela's eyelids burst open. Something was wrong. But what? That's when she heard voices.

"Art Campbell said a man and a woman pulled in just around sunset last night. I figured it might be you."

"Morning, Jasper. I suspected you might be here. Ain't that your stallion?"

"Yup. So where's the wife?"

"Pamela's still sleeping. What are you doing out in this weather?"

"Got caught in the storm, same as you."

Pam turned around under the hay and tunneled out of her cocoon. Mac knew Jasper's horse was here and he hadn't warned her?

She tried to see the men below.

Jasper walked over toward the stove. "Hmm, hmm, you're wife sure can cook. She did all this last night?"

"Obviously. I can't cook like that."

"What man can? Women are good for one thing, taking care of us men."

Pamela felt her temper rise.

"She ain't like Tilly," Jasper observed.

"Nope." Mac leaned against the wagon with his arms folded across his chest.

"I don't want to wake your wife, so I'll be going now. Too

bad we beat ya to the house. Mrs. Campbell keeps a mighty fine place."

"And I suspect it will stay that way," Mac countered.

Why was he saying that? Pamela shivered.

"Are you—"

"I wouldn't cross that line, Jasper. You know my reputation. I'd hate for you to experience it firsthand."

Jasper stepped back. He seemed paler. Was Jasper afraid of Mac?

"I hope the new missus doesn't fall victim to the same fate as the first." Jasper stormed out of the barn.

The first? Mac was married?

nine

Mac clenched his fist and released it. He'd hoped to get back on the road before Jasper learned they were in the barn. It had been quite a shock to discover Jasper's horse in the farthest stall last night.

The wind whistled through the boards as Mac tended to the animals. He'd have to deal with two realities today. One: More than likely they were stuck in Flatlick. Two: Jasper was heading west. He'd been staying ahead of them every step of the way.

Mac had kept the news from Pamela to give her some peace of mind. But how could he broach the subject? Jasper or one of his men would be back to check on their horses and, more than likely, to check on them.

Mac fed the horses fresh hay and water, then removed his Bible from the pack. Sitting down beside the woodstove, he closed his eyes and took in a deep breath. *Father, give me direction. I need to protect Mrs. Danner, and I'm not sure what I should do about the boy. Open Your Word to me, and open my eyes and heart to see where You're leading us.*

After his brief prayer, he opened the Bible and thumbed through the psalms.

"Whatcha doing?" Urias came up beside him and poured himself a cup of hot tea.

"Spending a little time with the Lord before we begin today."

With the mug halfway to his lips, Urias lifted his gaze and stared at Mac. "You believe all that stuff?"

"Sure do."

The young lad sat down across from Mac on the barn floor.

"How'd you sleep?" Mac asked.

"Great. Ain't been that warm for awhile."

Mac grinned. "I'm glad." He scanned the pages of the Bible and turned to the Twenty-third Psalm. *The Lord is my shepherd.* He mulled those words around. He'd read them so many times—repeatedly after Tilly's death.

Urias started wiggling his feet.

"Cold?"

"Nah, I'm fine." Urias sipped his tea.

Mac chuckled.

"What?"

"Nothing, just recalling how I had a hard time sitting still when I was your age."

Urias frowned.

Definite mistake—he'd just equated himself with the older generation. And Urias wanted very much to fit in with the adults. The boy had seen more and done more than most others his age, but he still was a child. Unfortunately, he wouldn't have the opportunity to escape adult responsibilities any longer.

Mac scanned the familiar psalm once again. *What am I missing? I trust God with my life. I trust Him with my needs. What is it I'm missing here?* He read on. "Thou preparest a table before me in the presence of mine enemies." Mac laughed.

"What?" Urias rose to his knees and tried to glance at the pages of the Bible.

"The verse I just read is: 'Thou preparest a table before me in the presence of mine enemies.' "

Urias flopped back down and squinted his eyes, tilting his head to one side. "You're a strange one, Mr. Mac."

Mac couldn't argue. "Tell me, do you belong in this barn, Urias?"

He looked toward the floor. "No."

"In one sense, you're Art Campbell's enemy because you haven't made friends with him and haven't obtained his permission to sleep in his barn. How would he know that you're not stealing from him? He'd see you as a thief, right?"

"I ain't stole nothin'," Urias defended himself.

Mac raised a hand. "No, Son, I'm not claiming you did. I'm just saying that's what he would think if he found you in here."

"I suppose," the destitute youth mumbled.

"See, that's what makes this verse kinda funny for you. You sat down at a feast last night in the middle of your enemy's barn. God provided and took care of you and even blessed you with good, hearty food in your belly."

Urias cracked a crooked grin. "And your enemy is Jasper?"

"Yeah, you could say that."

The boy chuckled, then sobered. "Don't think Mrs. Mac finds it too funny. She's crying."

"Crying, when?"

Urias whispered, "When I came down, I heard her. I didn't say nothin' 'cause I didn't want to embarrass her."

"Smart thinkin'. I'd better go check on Pamela." Mac left the Bible open on the crate he'd been sitting on. He climbed up the ladder and found nothing but the mound of hay. "Pamela," he called. *She wouldn't have gone out in this cold, would she, Lord?*

"Pamela," he called again. He kicked off the hay from the corner of the blanket and folded it over to the left side. He found her balled in the middle of the blankets, hiding. Crying. He dropped down to his knees and reached for her. "Pam, what's the matter?"

She refused to look at him. He caressed her shoulder. "Pam," he whispered. "Is it Quinton?"

Eyes blazing of fire stared back at him. Then he knew.

She'd heard the entire conversation with Jasper. She knew he'd kept a secret from her. And now she knew he kept two.

"I'm sorry," he fumbled, looking for the right words. "I didn't want to scare you. I hoped you'd get a good night's rest and we could get out first thing in the morning."

"I'm not a child," she spat back.

"I'm sorry. I was trying to protect you."

"I don't need your protection." Her words stung.

"Fine. I'll take you to Barbourville and you can hire another guide to take you the rest of the way." Mac stormed out of the loft and returned to the fire.

Urias was no longer in sight. Neither was his gun. "Great, just great." Mac dressed in his warm overcoat and slung his bow and arrows over his shoulder. *Where'd the boy run off to in this weather?*

ॐ

Pamela heard the barn door slam shut. Sleet and hail pelted the roof and sides of the barn. *Why would he go out in this storm, Lord? He wouldn't leave me here alone, would he?* She rolled her eyes heavenward and groaned.

She straightened up the loft, dusting off the hay from the wool blankets and folding them. Downstairs, she made a cup of tea and baked a loaf of bread. Toast, covered with peach preserves on the warmed slices, sounded wonderful.

Mac's Bible lay open on a crate. Picking it up, she closed it and moved it to the bench seat of the wagon. She noticed his pack was still there. Her shoulders relaxed. He'd be coming back. *Then where did he go?*

The boy. "Urias?" She scanned the entire area.

"It's freezin' out there," Urias said, squeezing through the loose board and wiping the sleeves of a tattered wool jacket two sizes too big for him.

"Where were you?"

"I had to. . ." He looked down at his feet. "You know."

What could he possibly have to do in this storm? "No, I don't. What is so important that you'd go out in this weather? And why did you use the loose panel?"

"You know, morning stuff," he mumbled.

Then it hit her. The very need she had herself and had been putting off as long as possible. "Oh." She felt her cheeks flush.

"Why didn't you use the door?"

"'Cause old man Campbell could see me. And it ain't like I've been invited to use the barn."

"Oh." The child had a point. "I'm baking the bread and planning on fixing myself a couple slices of toast with peach preserves on them. You're welcome to have some. I'll fix us some bacon and eggs when I return."

"Buckle up and cover your face. The wind's blowing the ice real hard," Urias warned.

"Thanks for the tip."

"Welcome." He sat down with anticipation. She dressed and opened the door. A wave of arctic air stole her breath. Pulling her coat tight, she stuck her hands under each arm. Leaning into the wind, she struggled to make it to the outhouse.

When she returned to the barn, she discovered Urias had set a pot of water on the stove to warm and had removed the fresh loaf of bread. "Thank you, Urias."

"Welcome. Figured you'd like warm water. The barn and stove help, but it's still cold in here."

"Yes." She lifted the canvas over the back of the wagon. She prayed they had enough wood for the rest of the day and evening. They could purchase some from the Campbells, but who would want to go out and collect it? She shivered just thinking of the short trek to the outhouse.

With little effort, she had the bacon sliced, a couple of

potatoes chopped and frying in the bacon fat, and eggs ready to cook after the potatoes were done.

Urias returned from taking apart his bed. "Smells great. Where d'ya suppose Mr. Mac went?"

"I don't know."

"You two fight often?"

Pam gave a quirk of a smile. "More than I'd care to admit."

"Don't be too hard on him. Us men try to protect our women."

"Oh? Just how much did you hear?"

"Enough to know that it was the best time to visit the outhouse." He leaned closer to her. "I don't know what Jasper's problem is with Mr. Mac, but I can tell the man is afraid of him."

"I noticed that, too."

"'Course, Mr. Mac's the largest man I ever seen. When I saw him come runnin' at me, I almost wet my pants."

"My reaction wasn't too different from yours." Pam smiled, removing the hash browns. Each egg sizzled as she dropped it on the hot frying pan.

"He's a good man, once ya get to know him. Don't think I'd want to be on his bad side, though."

Pamela already was, and she ached to set things straight with Mac. She'd overreacted. He had a right to have a past. He should have told her about Jasper, but his past with his wife was none of her concern. After all, they weren't married as everyone thought.

The door creaked open. Mac entered, covered in ice, his long black hair laden with icicles.

"What happened to you?" She ran over to him and helped him out of his coat.

"I was looking for the boy." He shook as he stood resolute, staring at Urias.

"Me? Why?"

Pam noticed Mac's hands were blue. "Come warm up by the stove. I've fixed some breakfast. He went to the outhouse."

Mac closed his eyes.

"Sorry, Mr. Mac. You two were. . .well, it seemed like the best time to go."

Mac shook his head. Pamela picked off the ice as it started to melt from his hair and pant legs. "Sit down. I'll get you some hot tea."

Urias finished his breakfast and brought his dirty dishes to the small basin used for cleaning.

Pamela whispered in Mac's ear, "I'm sorry, Mac. I do trust you. I don't know what came over me."

➳

Mac's body stung from the cold as he began to thaw out. He reached to put his arm around her waist and bring her to his chest, then caught himself. "Knowing Jasper's warm next door doesn't set well with me, either." He winked.

"How long has it been since you trimmed this hair?" she asked.

"Ages."

"You don't know when your husband last trimmed his hair?" Urias asked.

Pamela's gaze locked with Mac's. She silently implored him to tell the truth.

"Pamela is not my wife. She's a recent widow. Her husband died a few days back on the trail. I came upon them right after the accident."

"But I thought. . ." Urias clamped his mouth shut.

"Most people assume like you. Even Jasper assumed, and we've been letting him hold that assumption for Mrs. Danner's protection."

"Ah." Urias looked at Mac, then glanced over to Pamela.

"But ya fight like you're married."

Mac roared. "Mrs. Danner and I can get into a good row every now and again."

"Your secret's safe with me." Urias went to the woodstove and tossed a couple fresh logs in it.

Pamela cleaned up the dishes while Mac ate the semiwarm food quickly and drank two mugs of hot tea. Why hadn't he checked the outhouse before he ran off in the storm?

"By the way, the storm's just about blown its course. Down in the valley I could see the edge of the bad weather. I'd say another hour or two at the most."

"Should we get back on the road or wait until tomorrow morning?" Pamela asked.

"We'd have trouble making Barbourville before nightfall. I'm inclined to stay." Actually, Mac wanted to flee the territory and get Pamela as far from Jasper as possible. And he wasn't too comfortable about Jasper getting ahead of them. There were far too many places on the road where he and his men could jump them. "Urias, what are your plans, Son?"

"Ain't got none. I guess I'll head back toward Barbourville and try and find me some work."

Mac also didn't like the idea of the boy being on his own. "I have a winter cabin east of the gap. You're welcome to come and live with me."

"Really?" The boy jumped up. "You mean it?"

"Wouldn't offer if I didn't mean it. You can go on to the cabin and wait for me to return, if you like. There's plenty of wood cut, and if you hunt around the cabin, you'll find plenty of food. An old friend of mine, Black Hawk, is staying there right now. You won't be able to see him, so you'll have to yell out a message from me. Then he'll know you're free to stay there."

"I can do that. How can I find your cabin?"

"You can't. But I'll give you directions to some folks who know how to find it." Mac ruffled the boy's fire-red curls. "I'll teach you how to hunt and live off the land."

"I'd like that." Urias smiled.

"Good. But I need a favor from you."

"Sure, what can I do?"

Mac leaned down and placed an arm around the boy's shoulders and in a low voice told Urias his plan.

❧

As evening approached and the storm stopped, Urias went outside. Mac came up beside Pamela. "Pamela, I'm sorry I didn't tell you Jasper was here."

"Mac, I prefer to hear the bad news rather than be left in the dark."

"I understand."

Pamela reached out and took his hand. "What happened to your wife?"

He pulled his hand away. "You heard?"

"All I heard was something akin to a threat about your second wife meeting the same fate as the first. And seeing how Jasper thinks I'm the second wife, I'm kinda wondering what he might have in mind."

Mac took a step back. "Jasper had nothing to do with my wife's death." He could feel his chest rise with each intake of breath. *Calm down. Relax.* Closing his eyes, he took in a long, deep breath and let it out slowly.

Pamela reached out and placed her hand on his forearm.

"Mrs. Danner, I think it best if we don't go further with this discussion."

"Why are you afraid to talk about your wife's death?" she asked.

Mac counted to three. "Why do you avoid talking about your husband's death?"

Pamela blanched.

That should stop this dangerous discussion.

Mac stepped away just in time to hear a scuffle going on outside. He went to the door and opened it and saw Jasper holding Urias by the collar. "This thief says he's with you." Jasper kept the boy at arm's length. Urias tried to wriggle out from his grasp.

"He's with me. You can let him go. What did he steal from you?"

"Nothing, just caught him snooping around the Campbells' house."

"I wasn't doin' nothin' wrong, Mr. Mac, I swear." Urias took a step toward Mac and ducked when Mac reached out to him.

He's been beaten more than once. Mac had seen the signs earlier, but this confirmed it.

"Heading out, Jasper?" Mac asked casually.

Urias let Mac loop his arm across his shoulders.

"Yeah, work's a-callin'. Heard some Injins left the reservation. Good bounty in catchin' 'em. Ain't no man better than me for trackin' in these mountains."

Mac held back his judgment. Jasper and his men left a trail wider than a herd of buffalo. He gnawed his inner cheek. *So, how'd I miss it?* "Good luck."

"Ain't no luck. Pure skill." Jasper barked out an order for his men to saddle up. As soon as they went inside, Mac whispered to Urias, "Did he hurt the Campbells?"

"No, Sir."

"Good. Go inside and protect Mrs. Danner. I'm going to make sure the Campbells are fine."

Urias slipped through the door while Mac strode toward the long front porch of the farmhouse. Art met him out front as he approached. "That kid with you?"

"Now he is. Been spending a few nights in your barn. Anything missing?"

Art grinned. "Nothing that me and the missus didn't leave for him to find."

Mac chuckled.

"We're fine. Jasper even paid two bits. Helped that more folks were staying and that you were in the barn."

Art sobered without warning. "He says you killed your wife."

ten

Pamela woke for the second morning in her cocoon of hay. This day, however, started with greater promise. Jasper was after Indians, and she and Mac were on good speaking terms. Good terms about everything except the subject of his wife's death. Her own deception added to the limitations of their honesty. But what did it matter? This was a temporary union, a business arrangement. In a couple weeks she would say good-bye and never see him again. Though, admittedly, it would be a much nicer trip if they remained cordial.

She primed the woodstove and started the bacon and the last of their eggs cooking. Normally she bartered with the folks she stayed with for additional food, but the Campbells didn't appear to be the friendly sort. Even after Jasper and his three men left, they didn't invite Mac, Urias, and herself in. *Odd,* she'd thought at the time. This morning she was even more certain of it. What had Jasper said about them to make the Campbells so nervous? It didn't matter. The barn was comfortable and, without the ice storm, actually quite warm.

Breakfast ready, she took two quarters from her purse and proceeded to the big house. As she approached, a young couple came out. "Morning," they said in unison.

"Good morning. Is Mr. or Mrs. Campbell in?"

"Missus is in the kitchen. Can't say where Mr. Campbell is," the young man, around her own twenty-three years, replied.

"Thank you."

Pamela knocked on the front door and waited. The shuffle

of feet sounded behind the door before it slowly opened. "Can I help you?"

"Mrs. Campbell?"

The short, stout woman with gray hair nodded.

"I'd like to thank you for the use of your barn and give you a little something for the hay our horses ate."

"Ain't necessary." She reached out and took the money. Pamela suppressed a grin.

"Thank you again. You've been most kind."

Mrs. Campbell knitted her eyebrows together, then relaxed them. Looking to her left, then to her right, she leaned toward Pam and motioned with her forefinger for her to come closer. "You be careful, young lady. I hear your husband killed his first wife."

"What?" The question slipped out before Pamela realized she'd spoken.

"Mr. Smith, he said so."

Pamela shook her head. "Mr. Smith is not who he appears to be, Ma'am. Mac actually had to keep a watch on you folks to make certain he didn't rob you. But it's one man's word over another, I guess. Good day, Mrs. Campbell, and ask folks about Nash MacKenneth, Mac, as he's known by most. I wager you'll hear a very different story."

"That's just it, Dear. We have heard rumors about the crazy mountain man who killed his wife because she wanted to leave and return to the city."

Pamela felt dizzy. It couldn't be true. It just couldn't. She didn't say a word but walked straight back to the barn and sat down on the wagon's bench seat. *Was Mac the man she felt in her heart? Or was he the man who others apparently believed him to be?*

Yea, though I walk through the valley of the shadow of death, I will fear no evil: for thou art with me; thy rod and thy staff they comfort me. Father, God, give me strength.

"Pamela, are you all right?" Mac asked.

"Fine. I just want to leave."

"All right. Urias, it's time to go."

The gangly redhead climbed down from the loft. He wore new clothes. They didn't fit quite right, but at least they weren't torn and tattered. *Where'd he get those?* she wondered. Seeing him dressed in rags had made her wish she had kept some of Quinton's clothing. Quinton. . . It seemed like an eternity had passed since last she saw him alive.

They scrunched up together on the bench seat. Mac slapped the reins. "Yah," he commanded, and off they went back to the road, heading northwest and closer to Creelsboro.

But each stride of the horses took them further from the revelation. She didn't want to believe it. She couldn't. Her life depended on the fact that it was false information. Her heart beat with a passion to know the truth. Could she ever fully trust this stranger?

No. She'd have to stay on guard, watching his every move and, most importantly, guarding her heart, for little by little, mile by mile, her heart had softened toward Mac. *Lord, I wish I'd never gone to speak with Mrs. Campbell today.*

Death was all around. The trees were bare; the ground was frozen brown. Nothing shouted life.

"Mrs. Danner. Mrs. Danner." Urias nudged her.

"Sorry, what?"

"I said it's amazing that Mr. Mac got these clothes from the Campbells."

"Yes, yes, it is. Are you staying warm?" It seemed an awkward question. The ice storm had vanished and with it the unseasonably colder weather.

"Definitely." His freckled face beamed. The child within the boy emerged once again.

"Are you all right?" Mac put his arm around her. She stiffened. He promptly removed it.

"I'm fine. Just eager to get to Creelsboro."

They meandered down the road, catching glimpses of the Cumberland River. The water seemed ice free. Little remained of the storm, though a few saplings still remained bent from the strong wind and ice. The damp ground provided another testament to the storm. Pamela prayed they would make it to Barbourville and find some dry, clean beds. Cold, damp ground and living with a growing suspicion of Mac didn't appeal to her in the slightest.

The road shifted to the left as they traveled around the foothills of a mountain. "Urias, it's time."

"Yes, Sir." Urias took the reins, and Mac jumped down from the wagon.

"Keep your rifle cocked." Mac waved and headed straight up and over the mountain. He moved so swiftly and quietly, Pamela shuddered at the thought of this hunter coming after and killing his own wife.

Urias turned to her. "Why don't you trust Mr. Mac?"

"I trust him."

"Not really. I've been on the run for awhile now, and my home life wasn't what ya call normal. But I've learned to read people pretty well. Mr. Mac, he's a straight shooter. Liars and frauds have a way about 'em. Some can't look ya in the eye—they're the easiest to spot. Other's look you in the eye and dare ya not to believe 'em. Mr. Mac, he looks ya straight and he listens."

Pamela considered his words. He seemed too wise for a boy his age.

"Now, Mr. Campbell," Urias continued, "he's an interesting one. I'm not sure if I can trust him or not. The Campbells seem like good folks, but they were easily fooled by Jasper.

Anyone with half a brain ought to be able to see that man coming a mile away. Did ya see his sidearm? Now he's a man to watch out for."

Pamela thought back on Mary Turner and how confident she'd been with her love and respect for Mac. The woman had opened her home to her, a virtual stranger, because of Mac. Perhaps it was wrong to listen to the ramblings of Mrs. Campbell. After all, Jasper had fueled her doubts and worries about Mac. And now she'd fueled them in Pam.

"Thank you, Urias."

"For what?"

"Setting me straight on a few things. Do you think this plan of Mac's will work?"

"If Jasper's plannin' what Mac thinks he is, yup. Question is, can Mr. Mac get in position first?" Urias slowed down the horses.

Pamela held the edge of the bench seat. *Please God, be with Mac.*

❧

Mac's breaths matched each of his strides. The thawing ground made the run more difficult. He prayed old man Brown was still alive and kicking. If his plan were going to work, he'd need the reinforcement. He had two hours to get ahead of Jasper and his men.

The scent of an oak fire hit him before he could make out the cabin. A sigh of relief washed over him.

"Isaiah Brown, you in there?"

"And who'd be callin' my name?"

"Mac."

"Only Mac I know has a friend I know. What be his name?"

What had Isaiah so scared? As a freed Negro, he'd always feared someone would try to steal his papers and bring him back into slavery. "Black Hawk," Mac replied.

Isaiah opened the door. The sun reflected from his nappy crown of salt-and-pepper hair, and he gave a deeply wrinkled grin to his visitor. "It's good to see you, Mac."

Mac extended his hand. "It's good to see you, too. But I need your help."

"What's the problem?"

"I suspect Jasper and his men are going to ambush me and a lady he thinks is my new wife on the western side of the bend."

Isaiah's forehead furrowed.

"I'll explain later. Can you help?"

Isaiah lowered his voice. "I's got runaways in my cabin. Don't feel right leavin' 'em."

Mac knew Isaiah would put up any slave running for his freedom, and he supposed word had gotten around as to where to find the man. "I understand. I can't stay—I need to get into position. I have a young man driving the wagon around the bend. I'm hoping to catch Jasper in the act from behind."

"Tell ya what I can do. I'll send my boy over to Johnny Fortney, and I'll join ya when I can."

Mac knew that meant squirreling away the runaways. One didn't ask questions. It was best not to know. Then you couldn't lie in court if something ever came up against Isaiah Brown.

"Thank you, my friend. Perhaps we can do some naybob-bin' when I'm coming back through."

"Be nice chewin' the fat with ya." Isaiah waved.

Mac ran at full steam. He'd be pushing it to make it there on time. Hopefully, Urias had held back the horses some. Bobbing tree branches left and right, Mac forced his concentration level on where he was going rather than on what might be happening down the path.

Breathing heavily, he slowed down at the ridge, his senses

alert. He didn't know if Jasper would send a man up there to watch or not. Few birds stayed in the area through winter, but enough remained in the area to help provide some indicator if people were stirring. As he suspected, no noise. In the distance he could hear the wagon. It was still moving. Cautiously, he moved in. He loaded his Kentucky long rifle, placed it over his shoulder, and positioned an arrow. Below he had a clear view of the road and the bend. The horses and wagon came into view.

His blood chilled. Jasper drove the wagon. Mac fired off the arrow as anger ignited him into a rage.

eleven

Pamela twisted her tied hands. The leather straps Jasper had used bit deep. Urias lay bound and unconscious on the ground beside her. Hot tears streamed down her face. Mac's plan had sounded so wise this morning. But Jasper had outsmarted him. He'd attacked them before they hit the bend. She prayed he'd come along soon.

Pam wiggled over to Urias. *Father, please don't let Urias die because of me.* The brave young man had fought well. He'd tried to fire off his rifle, but a whip came from behind and knocked him off the wagon.

Jasper's men had pawed her as they tied her up. In wicked laughter, Jasper had warned them that Mac was still out there and it would be best if they left his wife alone. *Father, I know You don't approve of lying, and You know I've not been telling Mac the entire truth, but it paid off with regard to Mac not correcting Jasper. I'm still safe.*

She refused to think of what might have happened if Jasper knew the truth. "Urias," she called.

He moaned.

"Thank You, Lord."

How far away was Mac? Would Jasper's men ambush him? She'd seen only three of them. She scanned the ridge looking for the fourth man, but to no avail. Jasper had ridden off with her wagon very pleased with himself.

Something wasn't making sense. The Turners said no one could ever prove that Jasper and his men were at fault because he left no survivors. If that were true, why were she and Urias still alive? "Dear God in heaven, protect Mac."

Suddenly, she realized Jasper would return after he killed Mac. "Urias, wake up. We've got to get out of here."

❧

Mac slipped behind a rock after his arrow pierced Jasper's shoulder. Curses and commands passed the man's lips faster than a viper could attack. Only one man rode beside Jasper on the road. That meant two men were in the woods. But where?

He followed the ridge again. It was the logical choice for one man. A glitter of metal on the ridge proved his assumption. Mac took long and careful aim. When the dark form moved out from behind the silver gray rock, Mac fired.

He reloaded and looked for the man who had been on the horse next to Jasper. Following the left ridge, he found him slipping behind some undergrowth. Mac aimed and fired.

Two down.

Jasper broke the arrow in his shoulder and jumped down from the wagon, his gun in his right hand. "Come and get me, Mac. Your woman was mighty fine. . . ."

Mac closed his eyes and fought off the words that rushed into his mind. He breathed deeply. One man remained in the woods, unexposed. If he gave in to Jasper's taunts, he'd be killed.

"Before I killed her," Jasper taunted. "Come on, Mac. It's you and me now. Ain't it just the way you wanted it? You've been after me for a long while. Here's your chance."

Mac squeezed his eyes shut. Jasper couldn't have killed Pamela, he couldn't. *But Jasper kills all his victims.* All *of them. Forgive me, Lord.* Mac let out a scream and ran toward Jasper.

Jasper fired.

The bullet grazed Mac's arm. Pain fueled Mac's fury. "You're a dead man, Jasper."

Jasper's hands shook as he turned the barrel and aimed again. The shot whizzed past Mac's ear.

Jasper turned the barrel again.

Mac charged the last ten yards. His hands were around Jasper's throat before he aimed.

Jasper dropped his gun.

Mac released him.

Jasper coughed.

A shot rang out and Mac felt the bullet slam into his backside.

Jasper's lips curled in a wicked grin. "Thought you'd get the upper hand on me, huh?" He started to bend down and pick up his weapon. Mac kneed him in the chest. Reaching for the knife in his boot, he instantly had it out and at Jasper's throat.

In his anger, he'd forgotten the fourth man. He'd let himself be vulnerable. "Tell your man to back off or I kill ya."

"You're gonna kill me anyway," Jasper croaked.

"I'm not like you, Jasper. I'll turn you in to the authorities."

Jasper let out a snicker. "Yeah, like you let your first wife return home."

Mac felt his rage increase. He pressed the knife closer. "Tell him," he strained.

"We got him, Mac," a strange voice called from the woods. A young man with brown hair appeared with a rifle. Jasper's fourth man walked with his hands in the air in front of a rifle held by Isaiah Brown.

"Let him go, Mac," Isaiah said.

"He killed Pamela and Urias." Mac eased the pressure he'd been exerting on Jasper's neck with the knife.

"I'll bring them to Barbourville where he can be tried and hanged," Isaiah's young friend answered.

Mac nodded.

"The sheriff will want to hear from you, Mac," the young man added.

"I'll be there."

"I ain't hangin' for killin' 'em," Jasper's man protested. "We didn't kill 'em. They're off the side of the road back about three-quarters of a mile."

"Shut up, Wilson," Jasper hissed.

"I ain't hangin', Jasper. You wanna hang, go ahead. But I ain't hangin'."

"Go," Isaiah said to Mac. "I'll watch the wagon. I'm sure young Johnny can take these two on to Barbourville." Johnny bound Jasper's hands and searched for additional weapons.

Mac ran a couple of strides down the road, then broke into a limping lope. The bullet wound in his backside burned. Blood dampened the right side of his trousers. "Pam, Urias!" he hollered.

A cold sweat covered his body. "Pamela!" he yelled louder. "Urias."

The burn in his buttocks forced him to a slower limp. *Dear God, where are they?* He examined the road. He found the place where they had been overrun. Small droplets of blood appeared on the dirt path. "Pamela!"

"Mac, over here."

Thank You, Lord. His gaze followed her voice to his right. Soon he had them unbound and informed that Jasper was on his way to the sheriff's office in Barbourville. Urias seemed dazed but was coming around.

"Mac, you're bleeding."

" 'Fraid so. A shot glanced my arm."

"Your arm, my foot. The rear of your trousers is soaked with blood. Let me look at that."

"Not on your life."

Pamela stepped back.

"There's a doctor in Barbourville. We'll let him take care of it."

"All right. I'll go get the wagon."

"I'll get it." Mac released the tree he'd been clinging to for support.

"Put your foolish male pride aside. I'll fetch the wagon. You tend to Urias. He was out for quite awhile." She stomped off down the road without waiting for his response.

❧

"Of all the most stupid things," Pamela mumbled, working her way down the road. "The man's insufferable." A storm of emotions circled in her gut. Thankfully, Mac was alive and Jasper no longer posed a threat. He'd still have to explain how he got shot, not once but twice, and how he had time to get some other folks to come and lend a hand. She knew the man was fast on his feet, but he had had to trek up and over the ridge and back again. . . .

He won't be running for a little while. She giggled at the thought. *He won't be sitting, either.*

Laughter bubbled up to the surface. Big, brave Nash Mac-Kenneth shot in the buttocks—the irony was just too funny. She sobered a moment, considering how it must sting, then giggled again.

The sound of the wagon approaching caused her to pause. Had someone else come along and stolen it?

"Hello, Miz," an older black man called from the top of the wagon. "You must be Pamela. I's Isaiah Brown, a friend of Mac's."

"Hello."

"Where is he?"

She climbed up on the wagon. "Down the road a bit. He's been shot."

"I saw it. Thought I'd bring the wagon to him rather than having him walk back."

"He won't let me take care of it, says he wants to go to the doctor in Barbourville."

"Doc France is a good doctor, does a right fine job."

"Maybe you can get him to at least put a clean cloth to the wound and apply some pressure on it." Pamela folded her arms across her chest. "Why are men such. . ."

Isaiah laughed.

"What?"

"Women and men have been asking that question ever since Adam and Eve."

After Mac and Urias were loaded into the wagon as comfortably as possible, Pamela drove the two patients to the doctor in Barbourville. Isaiah stayed with them until they reached the path to his cabin. Pamela again was struck by the kindness of Mac's true friends. Unlike the Campbells, who hadn't known him, his friends showed no fear of the man. She really needed to trust her heart.

Mac lay on top of the canvas covering the crates. Urias alternated between lying beside Mac and sitting up. The boy's constant complaints about his headache worried her. Head injuries were always such a bad omen.

With the men lying behind her, Pam thought back on Angus's words of warning. She gripped the leather reins tighter. If only she had listened. Quinton would be alive. And Mac and Urias would be safe. Even Jasper and his men wouldn't have been tempted by the contents of their wagon. If only. . .

Bile rose in the pit of her stomach. She should have been stronger. She should have convinced Quinton it was wrong to chase their parents' dream. Who cares about wide, open spaces, a profitable store? Most would care to make a profit, but accruing wealth didn't matter if it meant losing everyone. She should sell the contents of the wagon in Barbourville, then send a letter to Elijah and Elzy Creel and let them know the misfortunes that had fallen on her family. Perhaps she'd ask if he'd resell the land and business for her. She couldn't run a business, at least not one her heart wasn't in. But what would she do in Barbourville after that?

If truth be told, Jasper didn't know the half of the contents in the wagon. In one trunk the entire family fortune in cash and gold lay safely hidden. If she were wise, she wouldn't have to work. But what would she do? She couldn't stay around an empty house all day. A boardinghouse, on the other hand, might keep her busy. Pam nibbled her lower lip.

Of course, there would be the increased work of doing the linens for her visitors. Pamela looked down at her hands. Additional laundry held no appeal, either.

I could teach, she reasoned. But Pamela knew she wouldn't have the patience with half a dozen youngsters clamoring for attention. No, teaching wasn't a real option.

You could marry. She grinned. The only man in whom she had been the least bit interested lay on the wagon behind her with a bullet embedded in his buttocks, and he didn't want her help. Marriage didn't seem like an option, either. Time. That was the problem. She needed time.

It hadn't been that long since Quinton died. Was she even done grieving the loss of her brother? She doubted it. There hadn't been time for anything except moving forward, avoiding the enemy—and still Jasper had almost won.

"We're nearly there," Mac murmured. She nearly jumped hearing his voice.

"How much farther?"

"A mile and a half. You'll find Dr. France's office. . . ." He rattled off the directions. Thirty minutes later, she found herself pulling the wagon up to a house. A real house. One with milled wood and glass windows. "These people are civilized," she squealed with excitement.

❧

Mac grumbled to himself. Humiliation burned deeper than the

wound on his backside. If he'd only been shot in a more appropriate place—if there were an appropriate place to be wounded. Dr. France teased him, but then quietly acknowledged that of all the places one could have been shot, this one did the least damage. The muscles would heal. Mac wouldn't sit down properly for a week, but he would recover.

Urias, on the other hand, had to be watched. His head still ached, but he was holding down his food—a good sign. Mac hadn't seen Pamela for hours. She'd dropped them off and left. He'd hoped. . . . What had he hoped? That she'd be there when he came out of the doctor's office? *Must be the whiskey, Lord.* He leaned against the wall as the room blurred. He closed his eyes and opened them slowly, trying to focus.

He blinked and realized he was lying face down on. . .on a bed with clean white sheets. "Ah, glad to see you're back with us." Dr. France grinned. "You'll need to stay down for awhile and drink plenty of fluids. Apparently you lost more blood than I was aware of. Your female companion returned and said she'd rented a room at a boardinghouse. I let her know that you and the boy will be spending the night here."

Mac raised his chest off the bed.

Dr. France placed a hand on his back and pushed him down. "Stay down and rest, give your body a chance to heal. Oh, the sheriff came by as well. You can visit with him in the morning. Something about giving testimony against a couple of bandits."

"Fine." Mac rolled over to his back. "Ouch!" He promptly rolled over and lay on his stomach.

Dr. France chuckled. "You'll be sleeping on your front or side for awhile."

He pulled up a chair and sat down beside him. "What caused those scars on your back?"

Mac clenched his jaw.

"Am I correct in assuming it's a bear? I'm guessing his paw spanned eight, maybe ten inches."

"Yeah, a brown bear. It killed my wife."

"I'm sorry."

"Ain't no one's fault but my own," Mac mumbled.

Dr. France rose from the chair. "Can it ever be anyone's fault when a wild animal attacks?"

Mac punched his pillow and buried his face. *Why did everyone always feel they had the answers to your personal issues? God knows and I know I'm at fault. I should have listened to Tilly. I should have taken her back. I should have. . .*

Should have and did were two different things. How many times would he continue to go down this path of blame? When would he feel the freedom of grace and peace again? When would he be whole?

"Mac," Urias whispered.

Mac turned his head to the left. "Yeah, Urias?"

"Doc has a point about your wife."

"Don't start with me, Boy."

"Sorry." Urias rolled to his side and faced the wall.

"Urias, I'm sorry. I didn't mean to bark at you."

"Ain't nothin'." Urias didn't roll back over.

"Come on, speak your piece. You've got something to say, spit it out. I'm a man, I can take it." *Most of the time,* he reminded himself.

Urias rolled back over. "I'm just guessin', but did your wife go out when ya told her not to or to a place ya told her not to?"

Mac raised his eyebrows. "How'd you know?"

"Fits. I mean, women, they don't listen."

Mac chuckled. "And how do you know this?"

"My ma. She wouldn't listen to anythin' Pa and I would say to her. Not when it came to her drinkin'. Anyway, I seen it other times, too. Men tell the women to do one thing, and they go and do another."

Not all women. At least Mac felt pretty certain they weren't all like that. "Can't judge all the women by one. Look at Mrs. Danner, she listens."

"Maybe. I don't know."

Mac rolled to his left side. His arm hurt, but it was bearable. "She's done a fair job following my instructions. Tilly, that's the name of my wife, she didn't want to live in the wilderness. We had an argument about it, and I left to go hunting for awhile. I found out she really didn't love me. She loved my parents' farm. And since I'm the oldest son, she figured I'd inherit the farm. Which I will one day, but I'm not ready to settle down there yet."

"She married you for your parents' land?"

" 'Fraid so. Hurts a man's pride, ya know. Anyway, Tilly decided she'd had enough and set out on foot to return home. She never made it. I heard her screams, but I was too late. I was so angry, I fought the bear and killed it."

"But she'd still be alive if she'd listened to ya and stayed by the house."

"Possibly. Hard to say."

"Seems to me, a man who believes the Bible like you do ought to have forgiven himself. Ain't much a man can do with a strong-headed woman. I know. Pa tried. Me, I've decided to keep women at a distance. Admire their looks some and their cooking but keep them as far away from my house as possible."

Mac laughed. "Son, when love hits, there ain't a man alive who can stand up against it."

"Ain't gonna happen. I'll live in the mountains like you. I should be able to avoid most of them that way." Urias nodded for emphasis. "Ouch."

Mac snickered. Then it occurred to him. He'd secluded

himself in the mountains for the very same reason. He didn't want to be affected by women again. And what happened? God put a woman on his doorstep. He flopped back to his stomach. Images of the beautiful widow played in his mind. *She's untouchable, Lord. Remove these thoughts from me.*

twelve

Pamela eased out of her feather bed and stretched in the sunlit room. She'd loved every minute of the past three nights she had spent in Barbourville. The townspeople, she found, were very friendly. Mac's and Urias's injuries were minor, and a few days of rest were the doctor's orders. Many hours she'd spent alone, thinking and praying for direction. Last night, as she pored over the facts and figures in her father and brother's ledger, she'd decided to try to sell the merchandise to the Croleys' store. Today she'd take the wagon from the stable and drive it there.

She'd taken inventory at the store yesterday and decided which items would be the most marketable. These were the items she'd pitch first. The second list contained fancier items, less practical, but still useful. The third list—she wondered why they'd even brought such useless niceties along. These she would continue to use on the road as thank-you gifts to those who helped them. Something to make a woman feel special or to give the house a touch of beauty. She found wilderness women enjoyed fancy things just as much as women in the cities back East. Here, however, the women were more pragmatic. If you don't need it, don't waste the money on it. It seemed just about every item in the kitchen served more than one purpose.

Dressing for a day of business, she folded the ledger shut and made her way to the dining area.

"Good morning, Pamela, did you sleep well?" Elizabeth Engle asked, her gray hair perfectly in place. It was hard to believe the woman was seventy-five years old.

"Wonderfully, thank you, Mrs. Engle."

"Breakfast is ready. You'll have to serve yourself this morning. I'm off to the market for some fresh winter squashes. I heard the Pitzers brought some in yesterday."

Pamela smiled. She knew the older woman had her own garden but probably couldn't keep up with the amount of food her boarders consumed. Elizabeth Engle was the perfect hostess and a wonderful cook. Pamela had felt at home minutes after she first arrived.

Mac and Urias had stayed one night at the boardinghouse, then decided to take a room closer to the stables. Fancy linens, curtains, and such scared them, which Pamela found incredibly funny in comparison to the no-fear attitude they held toward Jasper and his men.

The circuit judge had come and gone. Mac had given his testimony; Jasper had denied it. Urias had given his testimony, and once again Jasper denied it. She'd been prepared to give testimony as well, but the lawyer decided "to spare a woman the harsh realities of the courtroom." She'd held back her laughter on that one. Hadn't she already lived through the actual threats associated with Jasper? Could the courtroom even compare? The prosecuting attorney also had the statement from Johnny Fortney. When Jasper's partner decided to testify against him for fear of going to hell, the judge found no reason to continue the trial. Jasper was sentenced to die by hanging on Saturday.

Resolved not to watch the man hang, Pamela needed to finish marketing her wares this day or she would not be able to avoid the center square tomorrow, hanging day. If the sales went well, there would be room to put a bed in the wagon on Saturday and continue their travels, although it would mean they'd have to leave on Sunday. Mac's inability to sit for long periods of time and the constant banging from the bench seat convinced her she needed to lighten the load. She also had decided to have the wagon framed and covered. The storm they'd traveled through a few days earlier proved there needed to be more shelter in the wagon.

The stable was more than happy to do the modifications. Mac protested but finally conceded it was her wagon and ultimately her decision. Pamela knew enough about men to understand that more than his backside had been injured. His pride had taken a substantial blow, as well.

She walked down the street toward the stable. Mac walked with a slight limp toward her. "Good morning, Mac. Did you sleep well?"

"Fine."

What has him all upset this morning? she wondered.

"Look, I ain't goin' to beat a dead horse here, but are you certain you want to do this?"

"Yes, it's practical."

"But. . ."

She held up a hand to stop his protest. "Mac, I've gone over the figures. I'll still make a profit."

His eyebrows rose.

So, he doesn't believe a woman can handle simple mathematics. She untied the leather folder. "Here, look at these figures." She pointed to the column marked "purchase."

"Compare them to. . ." She slid her finger across the page. "These." She paused a minute to let him absorb the figures. "As you can see, I will still make a profit. Granted, it won't be as high as it would be if I sold the items individually, but then I would have to add in time on the shelves. Is the profit truly greater?"

"Uh. . ." He fumbled for his words. "Your husband did this before he died?"

"No." Her voice rose an octave. "I did this last night." She unfolded another piece of paper that listed the items in the three columns. "Here in column one you can see what is more likely to sell, and column two lists what might sell. The third column is hardly worth mentioning to Mr. Croley. It isn't likely he'd be interested in those items. I reckon most folks won't, either. They're dust collectors on a store shelf. They look pretty, but they aren't practical for wilderness living. If a man has some extra money, he might buy a gift for his wife. But that doesn't seem all that likely to happen. I imagine I'll have most of these items five years from now still gathering dust on my shelves."

Pamela knew she'd have very little stock in the store when she arrived, but the orders Quinton had placed before they left should arrive about the time she reached Creelsboro. Her stomach tightened. *Why does this happen every time I think of this place, Lord?*

Mac removed his coonskin cap and scratched his head. "I'd say you've got a head for business."

"Probably not. I've decided to give the items in column three away to individuals as thank-you gifts along the trail."

"I need to speak with you about the trip."

"All right. Can we speak after my negotiations with Mr. Croley?"

"That will be fine. Meet me at the hillside near the ferry."

She knew he liked that view. You could see down the Cumberland River and look at the mountains toward the gap. "Fine. Where's Urias?"

"Looking for work. I must say, the boy has a good sense of needing to provide for himself."

"I think he's been doing that for awhile." She leaned in closer to Mac. "I've purchased a set of clothes and a pair of boots for him. I just haven't figured out how to give them to him. Maybe you could ask him to do some things for me, and I could give them to him as payment."

Mac smiled. "I'll see what I can do. You think I'm doing the right thing, having the kid live with me?"

Pamela fought the desire to wrap herself in his arms and

hug him. "I think you'll be a very good influence on him." One of the things she'd been thinking over the past couple of days was her growing attraction to Mac. She trusted him, but she still feared telling him the truth. Her fear had changed from her original concern for her safety to his uncompromising sense of right and wrong. He'd feel lied to. No, she couldn't tell him the truth, at least not yet.

❧

Pamela Danner continued to surprise Mac. Not only had she endured the hard travel without one word of complaint, now he wondered if his original concerns regarding her ability to run a business were ill founded. *She obviously can work with numbers,* he acknowledged.

Mac squatted by the river and watched the current play. A small eddy formed every now and again, traveling downstream and popping back up again. Staying still and recovering, as Dr. France put it, was driving him crazy. He had to get back to doing something, anything. Inactivity would lead him to become stagnant like a lifeless river. Mac felt a bond between himself and the Cumberland. He needed the freedom to move about, to keep moving. He stood, relieving the pressure on his wound.

"Mac!" Pamela waved as she headed toward him with a bounce to her step.

"The sale went well?"

"Very. Mr. Croley purchased just about the entire stock."

"He keeps that much cash on hand?" *How much money passes through a store in the course of a couple days?* he wondered.

"Of course not. We bartered some, and he'll be making some payments."

"Payments? To where?"

She looped her arm around his. "I set up a special fund."

"Here? Are you planning on staying around?"

Pamela sighed and removed her hand. "No, but one bank is as good as another. And for the time being, this will work just fine."

"Forgive me for telling you your business, but how are you going to be aware of whether or not he makes his payments?"

"The bank will post me a message."

"And what will you do should he not pay?"

She scrunched up her nose and placed her hands on her hips. "I seem to be not understanding your logic, Mac. First you tell me the wagon is too full, and now that I've taken care of that problem and added some accommodations in the wagon, you're telling me I'm messing up again."

Mac squeezed his eyes closed and pinched the bridge of his nose. "I don't know if you realize it, but that's a lot of money you've put into a bank that you'll never be by again."

"Mr. MacKenneth, you can be the most stubborn of men that I've ever laid eyes on. And just so you understand I know more than you think I do, I realize exactly how much money is involved here. And I–I—" She clamped her mouth shut. "I've taken the appropriate steps to make certain my interests are protected."

Mac raised his hands in surrender. "I ain't goin' to argue with a woman about money. Just wouldn't seem fair."

Her face reddened. "I suppose you know exactly how much money you have in your savings, in your pocket, and in investments."

"More or less," he defended. Truth was, he wasn't certain how much money he had. He didn't count it all that often. He had some in his parents' house, in his cabin, and in the bank. In his pocket he kept some, but not much, and what he did have was nearly gone.

"Well, I can tell you down to the last penny where mine is and how much it is."

He could swear she was about to stick out her tongue at him.

"Fine. I didn't ask you to come over here to argue. I wanted to ask you about moving on. I can travel some, and I don't want to hit any more bad weather."

"Fine, when do we leave?"

"In the morning."

"Wonderful. I'll see you then." She turned and marched back to the center square of the town.

He rubbed his chin, thankful he'd kept his mouth shut about her feminine attire. She'd been wearing fancy dresses every day—not that she looked bad in them. He'd wanted to ask if she'd purchased a real pair of boots to travel with, but he didn't dare. He looked down at her fleeing feet and groaned. She had to have the prettiest set of ankles he'd ever seen. *Lord, help me deliver her to Creelsboro. . .fast.*

Mac turned and looked back at the river. The Twenty-third Psalm replayed in his mind and stopped at, "He leadeth me beside the still waters." He blinked, focusing on the river once again. The next verse he recited more slowly. "He restoreth my soul." He knelt down. *Am I constantly running, Lord, so that I refuse to hear what You're trying to say?*

Listening for some sort of response, he waited a bit longer. A bird sang in the nearby trees. A gentle breeze stirred the dry leaves on the ground. The river even played its music, but not one word from God. Mac wanted answers. He demanded them. But they weren't coming, and after all these years, he wondered, should they have come?

He got up and stomped toward the stable. He'd better give them a hand and make certain that wagon was ready to roll in the morning. *I need to keep moving, Lord.*

"Did you find Mrs. Danner, Mr. Mac?" Urias asked as he entered the stable.

"Yup. We're leaving in the morning."

Urias lifted a crate from the wagon and placed it on a nearby buckboard.

"What are you doing?"

"Mr. Croley hired me to bring over the items he bought from Mrs. Danner."

"That's great. I'm glad you found a job."

Urias grinned. "I don't think Mr. Croley knows I know Mrs. Danner, but it doesn't matter. It's a job, and it'll give me some money."

Mac knew Pamela had a hand in getting the lad the employment, but he wasn't about to tell him. "A man needs to work for his hire. Do you need a hand?"

"No thanks. I'm just about done." Urias dusted off his hands and leaned toward Mac. "Hanging is set for noon."

"We'll be long gone before then."

Urias's red hair gave a single nod. Neither of them was anxious to see a man hang.

"Is the work done on the wagon?"

"Just about. I think they're having trouble building the bed the way Mrs. Danner ordered it."

"I still can't believe she's insisting on a bed."

Urias laughed. "You two definitely look at life differently."

Mac grunted.

Urias laughed harder.

ﻚ

Pamela let out an exasperated breath. Why did she and Mac squabble so much? She opened her drawstring purse and pulled out a small trinket. Mr. Croley had said it was an actual Indian artifact and was supposed to bring good luck. She tossed it on the bed. It certainly didn't help her conversations with Mac. She'd been about ready to wring his neck for implying she was less than competent. Oddly enough, the more she felt attracted to him, the more his words stung.

On the other hand, she knew he'd be even more protective if he had any idea how much money she still carried in the wagon. She glanced over to her chest. The false bottom hid the family fortune. She'd worn each of her fancy dresses to keep up the illusion that she'd brought an entire wardrobe with her. Even though Jasper had been captured, tried, and convicted, she still didn't feel safe. If the residents thought Mr. Croley was paying the bank for his debt to her, they wouldn't be inclined to pursue her. One incident on the trail was more than enough.

Removing her social dress, she replaced it with a more comfortable one. Errands done, she wouldn't be going out again until morning. Tonight she would pack. Knowing Mac, he'd be here to pick her up before the sun crested the horizon.

An hour later, Pam's trunks were packed. She sat rocking in the wooden rocker Elizabeth Engle kept in the room. Pamela traced the curved line on the arm of the chair. Elizabeth had told her that her husband had carved the chair for her when she was expecting their first child. The rocking chair had been a real blessing over the years, Elizabeth said. She'd spent more hours in that chair rocking her fussy babies than she'd spent in any other chair in the house.

It still surprised Pamela how well furnished the home was. No question the late Mr. Engle produced quality furnishings. He'd made just about every piece in the house.

Pamela rocked back and closed her eyes. *Lord, I'm still in doubt about traveling on to Creelsboro, but I have no place else to go. Barbourville is tempting me to stay and make a home here. The people are friendly, but. . .*

Her mind drifted to the upcoming event in the town square. She knew justice had to be played out, but to know she was the reason a man had been hanged. . . . Pamela shook her head, hoping to clear the images from her mind's eye.

"Jasper killed many, Lord. I know that. And I'm thankful I'm still alive. I know he deserves his punishment for all those other people he's killed. I don't know; call me foolish, I guess. I just can't live where I know I played a part in the man's death."

A gentle knock on the door broke her from her prayers.

"Yes?"

"Pamela, Dear, it's Elizabeth. Are you needing anything else this evening?"

Pamela went to the door and opened it.

"No, thank you, I'm fine."

Elizabeth's matronly appearance of silver hair, gentle wrinkles, and warm eyes made it easy for Pam to open her heart to the older woman. "I must say, I'm sorry to see you leave so soon. You've been a most enjoyable guest."

"Thank you. I'll miss your hospitality as well. You've a beautiful home."

"Thank you. My Peter had a way with wood." The elder woman glowed.

Pamela's heart ached for that kind of a relationship. To be so close to a person that even in death you still feel a part of the other. She felt her eyes water.

"What's the matter, Dear?"

"Nothing. It's wonderful to see the love you still have for your husband, God rest his soul."

Elizabeth nodded her head and smiled. "I fell in love with Peter when I first set eyes on his handsome face. But love is hard work. It takes time and patience. It used to bother me that he spent so many hours making all this furniture. Then I realized—and I must say it took quite a few outbursts on my part before I understood—that making the furniture was his way of saying, 'I love you.'"

Pamela found it hard to believe that the very items the woman cherished had been the items they, as a couple, had fought over.

"Peter also realized that I wanted more time with him and not just with the things he made. Of course, that's when the idea hit to have me work with him on the furniture. The idea of sitting down, holding hands, and just talking was completely foreign to the man. But you're right, Dear. I do love him with all my heart. We had many good years together. And soon, I think, I'll be joining him."

"Are you ill?" Pamela worried.

"No, no, Dear. But remember, I'm seventy-five. I can't imagine living too many more years."

"I suppose you're right," Pamela mumbled. The older woman had been so open and loving that, earlier in the week, Pamela had found herself able to unburden to Elizabeth, explaining the lie she'd been living with for days.

"Oh my, I forgot. You've lost your parents and your brother in less than a year."

Pamela took in a deep breath and let it out slowly.

"I found comfort in the Twenty-third Psalm," Elizabeth offered.

"I've been thinking on that psalm a lot. I certainly have been walking through the valley of the shadow of death."

Elizabeth placed her blue-veined hand on Pam's forearm. "Read all the verses of that psalm, not just the fourth. There's a lot more there."

"There is?"

Elizabeth winked and patted her arm. "Good night, Dear. I'll see you in the morning."

"Good night." Pamela closed the door to her room, grabbed her Bible, and opened it to the Twenty-third Psalm. *What have I been missing?*

thirteen

Mac hoisted the last of Pamela's trunks into the wagon. She must have filled it with lead. Either that or the few days' rest had played more havoc with his muscles than he thought.

Inside he found Mrs. Engle providing a hearty breakfast for their departure. Mac ate in earnest, as did Urias. Pamela left the table early, claiming her need to arrange some items in the wagon. "Women," he muttered and forked some home fries.

"Thank you for the fine vittles, Mrs. Engle." Urias spoke with his mouth full.

"Pleasure. You take good care of Pamela Danner, you hear?" She shook her finger at Urias.

He sat up straight and responded, "Yes, Ma'am."

Mac chuckled. Mrs. Engle reminded him of an old school-teacher, very strict and very poised.

"And I expect you to do the same, Mr. MacKenneth."

Mac wiped his mouth with a linen napkin. "Yes, Ma'am."

Urias's face went red, holding back his laughter. Mac kicked his shin under the table.

"Hey," the boy cried out.

Mac winked. Laying his napkin beside his now-empty plate, he excused himself from the table. His mother would be proud, he thought.

Urias drank another glass of milk, grabbed a couple of biscuits, and followed Mac out the front door. Mac could hear Pamela shifting things around in the wagon. She had the flaps closed. *Should I knock?*

"Hey, Mrs. Danner," Urias called out.

She popped her head out through the opening. "Give me a minute."

Her golden hair draped down across her shoulders, and the blue of her eyes competed with the sky. Mac closed his eyes. "Take all the time you need."

Two minutes later, after what had seemed like an eternity, Pamela emerged through the front of the wagon dressed in her woolen traveling dress with a bonnet covering her beautiful hair.

"I'm all set, boys. Let's go."

Urias and Mac climbed on board. Mac discovered a small, long pillow covering the entire bench. "What's this?"

"Hopefully, it will help." Pamela looked straight ahead.

"Feels great," Urias piped in.

"It's nice to have you coming along, Urias, at least to Lynn Camp."

"I ain't got nothin' better to do. Besides, it's a long hike to Mac's place from here."

"You're welcome to travel the entire trip with us. I have more than enough provisions, and if we run out, I can always purchase more from the various farmers."

Mac looked over to Urias and nodded his consent. It might be nice to have the lad as a buffer between them.

A wide, toothy grin spread across the boy's face. "I would like that."

Mac slapped the reins. "Yah."

The wagon jerked forward.

"You know," Pamela said to Urias, "I'd like to talk with you about possibly working for me. I know Mr. Mac has offered for you to stay with him and learn to live off the land. And I know how exciting and important that kind of training is, but, well, I've been thinking, I could use a strong young man to help me at the store."

"Really?"

"You'd need to attend to your schooling, though. If you're to grow in the job, you'd need to know how to read and write. Not to mention how to add and subtract figures." Pamela glanced over at Mac.

Ouch! If the woman had daggers in those eyes, they hit their mark. He never should have questioned her figures regarding the merchandise.

Urias's shoulders slumped. "I'll have to think on it."

"We have time. Several days if I'm not mistaken, right, Mr. Mac?" She flashed her pearly whites at him.

"Right," Mac mumbled. She probably would be a good role model for the boy, so why did it bother him? Because he had felt a bond with Urias from the moment he caught him outside the Campbells' barn.

Hours passed, and Mac found himself lying on the bed he'd protested so strongly about, while Urias led the team. Even with the fancy pillow on the bench, his backside was hurting. He scanned the rearrangement of the various trunks. The heavy midsize trunk was in the front of the wagon to the right side, opposite the bed. He looked under the bed to see that Pamela had used every bit of space for storage. The woman continued to surprise him. He noticed she'd even purchased a pair of rugged boots for the trail. He suspected they were boys' boots, but he knew better than to bring up the subject.

"Whoa!" Urias halted the team. "Right here, Mrs. Danner?"

"This is wonderful, thank you."

"Why are we stopping?" Mac rose from the bed.

Pamela pulled the flap open. "Lunch."

She came inside and shuffled through the food pantry, as she liked to call it. She pulled out a bundle. "I prepared these this morning. I figured it would save us time today."

Mac nodded and accepted the sandwich, thick slices of ham and some cheese inside a bulky whole-wheat roll. "Thank you."

"Mac, we need to talk privately. I'm going to send Urias off for a bit," Pamela whispered.

Mac swallowed.

"Urias, Mr. Mac and I need to have some private words. Would you mind eating over there?"

"Nah, I may go farther. When you two have private words, you get loud."

Pamela's face reddened, possibly matching the shade Mac felt his own face turning.

"Thank you. I'll call you when we're through."

Mac felt the wagon bounce as Urias jumped off.

Pamela placed a hand on his arm. "Mac, I have a confession to make."

Pamela nibbled her lower lip. *How do I begin, Lord?* "Mac, I did a lot of thinking while we were in Barbourville."

Mac sat upright with his legs hung over the side of the bunk.

"I wanted to speak with you without Urias hearing because I wanted to speak about him."

"Yes, you seem to have planned out his future."

His words stung. "I'm sorry. I should have spoken with you first. I have nothing compared to the excitement you can offer the child. But what about his education? Surely you would agree he needs an education."

Mac rubbed his hands on his knees. "Yes, he needs an education. But books aren't all a man needs to learn. That boy has been beaten time and again. He needs to learn others don't do that."

"I know." She sat down on the crate across from him. "I think I can give him that if he comes and works for me."

He grasped her hand and held it lightly within his. The warmth of his hands calmed her. "Pamela, I know you mean well, but the boy needs a man in his life, too. A strong man who doesn't strike out at others for no reason, who doesn't bend and hide at the first sign of trouble." His imploring gaze locked with hers. "A man needs to be treated like a man. If he came to work for you, he wouldn't know if he was loved or just hired on."

"Of course I'd love him. If I didn't, I wouldn't offer him—"

He placed his finger to her lips. "Stop. Think, please," he pleaded. "Try and consider this from a man's perspective."

She thought of her brother, her father, and how they had approached problems, how they would focus on a single objective and go after it. *How does that apply to this?* she wondered.

"It's for the boy to choose, anyway," Mac continued. "We can't go deciding his future. He needs to decide on his own." He released her hand and grabbed his sandwich. "This is very good, thank you."

He's done it again. Just like that, he's dismissed me. Pamela's temper soared to the roof of the wagon. "I wasn't through talking with you."

"I'm sorry. What else did you wish to say?" Mac placed his sandwich back down.

"I hate it when you dismiss me like that. When you think you're all-knowing. Just who do you think you are, anyway? The world's number-one expert on anything and everything? Well, you better think again, Mister. Because there's one woman who sees through your pompous ways." She stormed out of the wagon.

"Pamela," he hollered.

She continued to walk away from the wagon and on past Urias. "Didn't go so well, huh?"

"That man is thicker than, thicker than. . .oh, I don't know. That rock, I suppose. I need to clear my head. Tell Mr. Rockhead I'll be back in awhile." Pamela continued to walk farther away from the road. The roar of water could be heard through the trees. She headed for the sound. Deeper into the woods she went. She'd planned to confess her secret as well, but there was no talking with the man. Just as soon as she allowed herself to start having feelings for him, he stomped all over her heart.

Tears streamed down her face. "Why doesn't anyone ever listen to me, Lord?" She pushed on and found the stream. Water danced lazily over broad, smooth stones, cold and refreshing. She dampened her face.

The Bible verses she'd read the previous night came to mind. *"He leadeth me beside the still waters."*

She looked at the stream. "This water isn't very still, Lord." Looking for some quieter water, she turned upstream. Calm would be a welcome relief. She walked until she reached a small pool, the water so clear she could see down to the bottom.

Pulling the small charm she'd purchased in Barbourville out of her pocket, Pamela sat down. "This isn't working." She raised her hand to pitch it into the pool but held back. The charm was a stone carving of a wolf.

"What do you have there?"

She yelped.

"Sorry, I didn't mean to scare you." Mac leaned against a tree.

She folded it in her palm.

"Pamela, why do we argue so?" He softened his voice.

"I don't know." Tears fought to the edges of her eyes.

"I don't mean to hurt you. I know I'm no good around women, which is why I keep my distance. But it seems every time we talk, we end up arguing. Why is that?"

"I'm sorry. I don't know. I've never had this problem with anyone else. I mean arguing. I've had other men not take me seriously. Like my father and brother when I warned them about coming west. They didn't believe me, and look where it got them. They're both dead."

"When did your brother die?"

She fumbled for an answer. "Not too long ago." At least she wasn't outright lying to him. Could her deceit be a cause of their constant problems?

"I'm sorry for your losses. Look," he said, noticing the pool behind her. "Beside still waters," he whispered.

Pamela looked back at the pool and back at Mac. "Twenty-third Psalm?"

"Yup."

Lord, are You talking to me through Mac? "Mac, I'm sorry we always fight, but do you realize you've never given me credit for knowing anything?"

Mac leaned against the large boulder by the stream. "I'm sorry. I guess in some ways you remind me of Tilly, my wife. We fought a lot before she died."

"I'm sorry. But Mac, I'm not your wife, and I don't know the first thing about your problems with her. I do, however, know a little something about the problems we've been having. For example, you didn't think I was capable in business. Truthfully, I'm not so certain I'll do a great job when it comes to handling money. But I do know some things. What you don't know is that one of my chests has a fake bottom in it with more money than you've probably seen in your entire life. It's the entire Danner family inheritance."

"What? What are you doing carrying that kind of money on you?"

"There was little choice. Quinton decided it was best."

"Woman, you're crazy. Do you have any idea what would happen if word got out about that?"

"All too well." She rubbed her neck, remembering Jasper's ugly paws on it.

Mac let out an exasperated sigh and pulled her into his embrace. "I'm sorry."

She leaned against him and savored his hug. "Mac, I left

the money from the sale in the Barbourville bank for that very reason. I didn't want to face another Jasper on the road, and I was certain word would get around about Mr. Croley purchasing my stock."

He leaned against the rock she had once been sitting on and continued to hold her. "I'm sorry, Pamela. I didn't realize. You're a wise woman, and you're right, I haven't given you credit."

"Thank you, Mac. That means a lot." She inhaled the deep musky scent that was all Mac. *Lord, help me, I could stay in this man's arms forever.*

A shot sounded from the direction of the wagon. Mac sprang up and ran. Pamela followed.

≈

Mac ran hard back toward the wagon. His wound protested. Urias sat backwards on one of the horses with his rifle aimed toward the covered wagon.

"What's the matter?" Mac cried.

The barrel of the rifle wobbled as Urias's hands shook. "A bear jumped into the wagon. It's a dumb one, too. He didn't leave when I shot the gun."

"Lower your rifle. I don't want you shooting me when I go in." Mac slipped to the backside of the wagon and pulled open the flaps, then moved to the front and pulled open the front flaps. A young bear stood on all fours eating either his or Pamela's sandwich. Who could tell? "Who cares?" he murmured. "Move on," he yelled at the bear, who merrily ignored him.

"You're right," Mac muttered to Urias. "It is a dumb bear."

Urias turned toward Mac and gave a full bow while keeping his perch on top of the horse.

The easiest way to handle this, Mac figured, would be to coax the critter out with some more food. Mac jumped down and went to the rear and opened the pantry. Pulling out a small ham, he unwrapped it and waved it in the air in front of the bear.

"What are you doing?" Pamela asked, catching her breath.

"A bear," Urias informed her.

She slid beside a tree.

Mac moved the ham slowly around the rear of the wagon.

"My ham?" Pamela's voice squealed.

"All for your safety, my dear." He smiled and continued to coax the bear.

The young bear licked the outer edges of his mouth, having finished the sandwiches, and sniffed the air. Catching the scent, he let out a soft growl.

Mac motioned for Pamela to work her way to the front of the wagon. The bear stumbled to the rear. "Come on, Boy. Come and get it," Mac urged. Thoughts raced through his mind. *Where should I toss it? To the side? But would I get enough distance? If I feed him, how long will he follow? If I throw it down the road, I could get more distance between us and the ham. But would the distance be great enough to keep him occupied for a few minutes?*

The front paws of the bear now grasped the back edge of the rear boards. Mac leaned the meat toward the bear's snout. "That's it, Boy, come on."

Raising his snout in protest, the bear growled, then lunged.

Mac tossed the meat down the road and toward the left, hoping it would convince the animal to return to the wilds rather than pursue them. Killing an animal for no reason didn't set well.

"Run!" he shouted to Pam and Urias.

Pamela jumped up on the wagon. Urias flew off the horse and dove in. Mac ran and leapt up into the rear of the wagon. Pamela had the reins in her hands in seconds. The horses didn't need any encouragement to run and took off hard. No one spoke a word. Twenty minutes later, Mac took the reins.

Slowing the team down, he encouraged Urias, "You can put your gun down now, Son."

The boy's white knuckles proved he was still concerned. "Will he come back?" Urias asked, not taking his gaze from the road behind them.

"Possible, but his belly should be full enough to give us some distance."

Pamela slipped inside the wagon. The memory of the warmth and softness of her resting in his arms brought back the fresh clean scent of her golden hair. Mac's heart fluttered. So wonderful were those feelings, he'd started to consider thoughts of kissing her. He didn't know whether to be upset or grateful for the intrusion of their furry friend. "A blessing," he muttered.

"What?" Urias asked.

"Sorry, I was thinking how young the bear was. That's a real blessing."

"Oh. Was it a young bear who gave you the scars?"

Mac groaned.

"I ain't goin' to tell no one. But seein' that bear made me remember your story. I ain't big enough to wrestle no bear and live, like you." Urias looked down at his feet.

"Let's hope you never have to. The bear I wrestled was much older." Mac swallowed a lump thicker than the regret he'd felt a moment before when considering his growing affections toward Mrs. Danner. *I suppose I could always pay her a visit next spring when I return. Creelsboro isn't too far from Jamestown, and perhaps the young widow might be ready. . . .*

What am I thinking? Lord, help me. You know I've sworn off women.

fourteen

Pamela stuffed the Indian charm back into her purse. She doubted it had any effect on what just happened between Mac and the bear. But another part of her couldn't help but wonder. She also knew that Mac didn't believe in such things, and his Christian faith seemed firmly rooted. *Am I that weak, Lord? Have I been playing games with You?* She considered Angus and the others. They'd always lived in fear. Mac was the complete opposite; he faced his fears. If she had heard Urias correctly, Mac's wife had died from a bear attack. *I doubt I'd be able to face another bear, Lord.*

She straightened the back of the wagon. The loss of the ham would change the meals she'd planned, but she knew Mac would hunt up something. She would not go hungry with him around.

The wagon bounced. She slipped and lost her footing. "Ouch."

"Y'all right?" Urias peeked his head in.

She didn't turn to look at him. "I'm fine."

Mac seemed to understand the boy. She wanted to help. Was it wrong to encourage him to get an education, to give him a job?

She reached for the canvas flaps to close the wagon's cabin. Exhaustion washed over her, and she lay down on the bed.

❧

"Hey, Sleepyhead, time to get up."

"Huh?" Pamela blinked. Her head felt like garbled wool just waiting to be spun.

135

"We're here." Urias smiled. "Mr. Mac said to wake you up. He's taken care of the horses. There's plenty of room in the tavern for us. And don't be fretting about that ham. Me and Mr. Mac will hunt us some food if we need it. But this place smells great."

Pamela sat up on the bed, adjusted her hair, and sniffed the air. Her stomach gurgled. The thought of not having to cook and to simply sit down at a fine meal pleased her immensely. "Thanks. Where are we?"

"Halfway to Lynn Camp. We should make it there tomorrow. I gotta go clean up." Urias jumped out of the wagon. "I'll see ya inside."

Her mouth dry and none too fresh, Pamela snipped a small piece of dried mint from her herb collection she'd brought along. The brittle leaf crunched, but its oils refreshed the palate.

The house had a large front porch that spanned the entire length of the building. A warm orange glow in the sky revealed tomorrow should be a very pleasant day for travel.

Pamela blinked going from the dim light outdoors to the even dimmer light indoors. A stout woman in her forties greeted her with a smile. "Welcome. Your menfolk already secured your rooms and let me know y'all be dining this evening."

"Hi. I'm Pam Danner." Pamela extended her hand.

The woman wiped hers on her apron. "I'm Bess Smith; Hyram is in the barn with your husband."

"Mac's not my husband."

"Oh, well, we don't—"

Pamela raised her hands to stop the woman. "Mac will be sharing the room with Urias. I'll be staying in the single room."

"All right." She creased her forehead.

"Mac's escorting me to Creelsboro."

"I see."

It was plain as the woman's face she didn't, but Pamela decided not to argue.

"Take a seat and I'll serve ya soon. Or you can go up to your room. It's the first room on your right when ya reach the top of the stairs."

"Thank you." Pamela decided to sit and wait for Urias and Mac.

Dinner proved very enjoyable once Mrs. Smith understood the circumstances of their traveling together. Of course, the woman now believed her guest was a recent widow. Her belly full, Pamela got up to stretch her legs before retiring for the evening.

"May I join you?" Mac asked.

"Sure. Urias, would you like to come?"

"Nah, I'm going to take in some target practice. Mac showed me a few things while you were sleeping."

"You fired a gun and I didn't wake up?" Pam knew she slept well but. . .

Mac chuckled. "No, though I'd wager you could have slept through it if we had."

"You were snoring." Urias laughed.

"I don't snore," Pamela protested, then promptly sneezed.

"Must be a cold coming on." Mac smiled.

Urias pushed himself from the table. "I'll see ya soon."

She watched him tuck his unruly red curls under his cap and exit the tavern. "He's an interesting kid."

"Yeah. I like the manners he's been showing, but I'm praying they aren't a way of trying to convince us he's something that he isn't."

"Is he old enough to be that deceitful?"

Mac helped pull her chair from the table. *What's this new behavior in Mac?* she wondered.

Pamela inhaled deeply as she stepped outside, the fresh air

a welcome relief. The tavern's heat and the odors from the cooking no longer seemed quite so wonderful now that she had a full stomach.

Mac walked beside her and folded his hands behind him. "Pamela, I want to apologize. I've been far too hard on you."

"I don't know what I'm doing out here. This is my father's dream, my. . .Quinton's dream. I never wanted to leave Virginia in the first place. And it didn't help any with Angus's warnings before we left."

They continued walking along the road. The stars sparkled like finely polished silver.

"Who's Angus?"

"An old slave who worked for my parents. He's been around all my life. He said he read it in the leaves."

Mac placed his hand on her and stopped. "I thought you were a Christian."

"I am." She looked down at her feet. "Look, I know most Christians say not to believe in such stuff, but I hear them saying and doing things all the time that show they really do. Like the number thirteen. Can a number be a bad number?"

"No, I don't believe thirteen is a bad number, and personally, I don't care what others believe. But I do care about you, Pamela, and I'd hate to see you trusting in what the Bible calls the elemental spirits of this world. There's no question some of these spirits have some sort of power, but I think people give them more power than they really have. I'd love to continue this discussion, but it's getting darker and we should return. Will you stay outside and sit on the porch with me?"

"All right, but my father and Quinton argued until they were exasperated with me."

Mac roared. "Well, we know I can get that way with you, too. Come on, let me explain my thinking on the matter."

Pamela slipped her arm through the crook of Mac's elbow

as he escorted her back to the house. *Lord, what's wrong with me? I love just holding on to this man.*

"I think you heard me mention Black Hawk, my Indian friend."

Pamela acknowledged his comment with a slight nod of her head.

"Well, Black Hawk had a religion that the Bible mentions as believing in the elemental spirits of this world. It's the one his ancestors taught him. His beliefs ran deep, very deep. I used to spend hours talking with him about God, the Bible, and the difference between the Great Spirit he knew and the Holy Spirit I knew. To make a long story short, it took stripping the man of his heritage, forcing him to live in a place he didn't want to live, before God got through to him. I'm not saying that means what we've done in moving the Indians west is right. I'm just saying that it was what the Lord used to reach Black Hawk. My friend could relate to the Jews who were taken from their land and used as slaves.

"I don't believe all this hardship comes just so you can learn to trust God, but. . ."

Pamela pulled the charm from her purse. "I bought this in Barbourville."

"Do you know what it is?"

"They said it was an Indian charm for good luck."

Mac grabbed the charm and huffed. "No, it's a fetish. It represents a spiritual guide in the form of a wolf to lead you."

"Well, once the bear was in the wagon, I knew it wasn't working."

"Answer me honestly, Pam. Would you really want the spirit of an animal guiding you rather than the Spirit of our mighty God in heaven?"

"Of course not." She sighed. *But isn't that what I've been doing?*

"You said your friend read tealeaves. Can the leaves of tea sticking to the bottom of your cup really say anything?"

"No. Well, I don't know. It's too hard to say. So many things Angus said over the years came true."

"I can't explain how that happens, but I know I serve a God who's real. He's alive and. . ." Mac paused.

Pamela reached out and grabbed his hands. "What's the matter?"

"I just answered some of my own questions."

"You? You have questions about God? I thought you were like a preacher, you know so much."

Mac chuckled. "Far from it. And I'm not perfect, Pamela. If anyone has seen that, it's you."

"What questions were just answered for you?"

"The last verse of the Twenty-third Psalm."

"You've been reading that, too?" *Does everyone read this psalm?* she wondered.

"For years, but I just understood what the first verse, 'The Lord is my shepherd,' is saying. The last verse concludes with 'Surely goodness and mercy shall follow me all the days of my life.' I mean, I wouldn't allow myself to live in God's grace because of blaming myself for Tilly's death."

"Mac, what happened to Tilly?"

For the next few minutes Mac described his relationship with Tilly, how they courted, married, and moved to the mountains. She didn't like living in the mountains and wanted to return home. Apparently, she'd never really loved him but had married him for the family inheritance she felt would be hers one day.

"I haven't spoken about this for a couple years now, and in a few short days I've spoke on it three, no, four occasions."

"I'm sorry."

"Don't be. I'd like to be friends, Pamela. I know I haven't

been the most sociable of persons, but you impress me." He fumbled with the charm in his hand. "You don't need this, Pam. You simply need to trust God, even when death encircles you."

Pam closed her eyes and bowed her head. In some far reach of her mind, she knew his words were correct, but she doubted she had faith that strong.

"I won't force you to throw this away. But I think you should." He placed it back in her hands. It felt heavy, cold, lifeless.

"Good night, Pamela. I'll see you in the morning."

She sat there for awhile and let the evening's words replay in her mind. If God was her Shepherd, did she need to believe in omens and elemental spirits? Identifying the omens, the Indian charms, or fetishes as "elemental spirits" caused her to rethink the matter.

An owl screeched.

Pam jumped up and went to bed.

🖘

Mac felt years younger the next morning as he harnessed the team. He'd spent his devotions praising God, at last reconciled to Tilly's death. She had known better than to leave the house. And she was responsible for her choices. Together, they should have worked things out. But he'd been so hurt by her confession that she'd only married him for the inheritance, he'd left her to fend for herself that day.

Second guessing, blaming oneself, didn't change reality.

"Good morning, Urias."

"You're in a good mood. Mrs. Smith says breakfast is ready when you are."

"Thank you. Tell her I'll be right in. Have you seen Mrs. Danner yet?"

"Nah, but the sun ain't up, either."

"Yes, it is. You just don't see it because the mountain is blocking it."

Urias yawned and stretched. "If ya say so. Iffen Pamela doesn't want to sleep on the bed in the wagon, I might just sleep in."

"What kept you up so late?"

"Nothin', really."

Mac looped his arm around the boy's shoulders. "Wanna talk about it?"

They headed toward the tavern's front door. "I don't know what to do. I like ya both. I want to learn to hunt and live off the land like you, but I, well, I don't know how to read so good. School ain't been held in high regard in my family. But I've seen you two reading all the time. I see Mrs. Danner working with numbers, and I know I ought to know them, too."

"You're right, a good education is important for a man. He can provide for his family wisely. And being able to live off the land can feed a family well. It's a hard choice. Perhaps you could do both."

Mac opened the door.

"How?"

"How, what?" Pamela smiled.

Mac grinned. Her golden hair, fair skin, and blue eyes set his heart pumping. *She has to feel it, too.* "Urias wants to live with you and me."

"What?" Pamela's voice squeaked.

"What I said," Urias explained as he sat down beside Pamela, "is that I want both educations."

"Ah." Pamela placed the linen napkin in her lap.

Mac sat down across from her.

"Mr. Mac says I can have both."

"How?" Pamela asked.

Urias chuckled. "That was my question."

"Easy." Mac sipped the hot tea from his cup. "The boy lives with you for a couple years. He'll get his education. Then he can come live with me. However, during the summer, I'd like him to live up on the farm in Jamestown. What do you think?"

Pamela looked at Urias. Urias looked at Pamela. Both smiled.

Mac clapped his hands. "Great! That's settled. Let's eat and get ourselves up to Lynn Camp before the sun sets."

Pamela opened her mouth to speak, then promptly closed it.

Feeling more confidence than he'd felt in a long time, Mac proposed another plan, one he favored. "Of course, there is an alternative, but I doubt it would work."

"What alternative?"

"Perhaps Urias could live with us."

fifteen

Shocked beyond words, Pamela finished her breakfast in silence. Hours later, sitting beside Mac on the jostling bench seat of the wagon, she continued her silence. Was Mac really suggesting they get married, or was he just teasing with his second alternative? After all, he'd said nothing about marriage. Even Urias, sleeping soundly now in the wagon, hadn't responded to Mac's second plan.

"Pam, I'm sorry. I didn't mean to be forward."

She blinked. However ridiculous his offer had been, it had met with serious interest on her part. How could she have fallen in love with a man she barely knew? It felt like ages since they had started this journey west, yet they weren't halfway to their final destination.

"I'm excited," Mac rambled on.

She continued to blink at him in amazement. Was he excited about marriage? *No! No, it can't be.* She closed her eyes and held them shut for a moment.

"At Lynn Camp there's a beautiful waterfall. When there's a full moon, a moonbow shines over the falls."

"A moonbow?" *What's a moonbow?* And how could she have confused Mac's excitement with her own wayward thoughts of marriage. *Lord, help me. How am I going to handle the rest of this trip?* she silently prayed.

"Yeah, the full moon's rays are reflected in the spray of the waterfall. It's an incredible sight. I've never heard of anything like it anywhere else."

"I would like to see it."

"Not tonight, I'm afraid. We have a new moon." Mac paused. "Pamela, I truly am sorry. I didn't mean to offend. I know you're a widow, and well, I just wasn't thinking."

How could she explain that her being a widow had nothing to do with it? Because she wasn't a widow. "Mac, I'm not—"

"Ouch!" Urias cried out.

"What's the matter?" both she and Mac asked in unison.

"I itch all over, and I've broken out with a bad rash."

Mac pulled back on the reins. Inside the covered wagon, they looked over the rash on the boy's hands and legs.

"Poison ivy," they pronounced together.

Urias raised his right eyebrow. "I itch real bad."

"I can see that," Mac said dryly. "You must have been shooting in a patch of the stuff."

"There were no leaves," he protested.

"Of course not. It's November. Strip to your underdrawers. Pamela, make some cool compresses and apply and reapply them over his skin. I'm going to hunt down some golden-seal root."

Thinking to ask him how he would recognize the plant without its leaves, she decided it would be a stupid question. "All right.

"Urias, call me once you're ready."

Relief washed over her when Mac returned. Urias had been very uncomfortable.

"Pam, do you have a—"

"Right here." She handed him the mortar and pestle she'd pulled out earlier.

"Thanks." Mac ground the mucousy roots to a relatively slimy substance. "A couple weeks back I could have gotten some jewelweed, which is much better for poison ivy, but the goldenseal root should work fairly well."

Pamela noticed he had brought more roots than he ground

up. Mac applied the yellow paste. "We're going to keep pressing on, Urias. But if you get too uncomfortable again, just holler."

"Thank you." The boy's eyes seemed swollen. Pamela prayed he hadn't rubbed them with his itchy hands.

"He's very sensitive," she stated.

"I've seen worse. He should be feeling better soon. But he'll be uncomfortable for a few days. He must have been shooting in a thicket of dormant vines."

As the day wore on, Pamela found herself enjoying her conversations with Mac. He actually had a lot to say once she managed to get him talking. Periodically interrupting their conversation, Pam would crawl back to reapply the goldenseal paste to Urias.

By evening they found themselves at Lynn Camp and made their campsite not too far from the waterfall. Urias held his hands and feet in the icy water above the falls as long as his body could stand it. The goldenseal was working, but the scratches in his skin from the dried vines meant he'd be weak as his body fought off the poison oil in his blood.

With the small tent she'd purchased in Barbourville set up, dinner prepared and eaten, and cleanup finished, Pamela found herself walking with Mac toward the falls. The rushing water roared as they drew near. "It's beautiful."

Mac's gaze caught hers. "God creates some mighty fine things."

"Upstream the water doesn't appear to be moving this fast," she noticed.

"The closer you get to the falls, the more rapid the water plunges over the edge. It appears to be about 125 feet across today. I've seen it in the spring when the snow's melting. It can reach three hundred feet across."

"You've been here often?"

He quirked a grin. "A couple times a year. It's on my way back and forth."

He leaned against a large boulder overlooking the falls. He'd drawn back his long black hair, making his rugged and handsome features more pronounced. Desire to reach out and hold him, to absorb his strength, washed over her like the cascading waters beside her.

She took a tentative step toward him.

Their eyes locked.

He leaned toward her, then coughed, breaking their connection. He turned back to the waterfall. "The descent of the waterfall changes during the year. I've seen the pool so full it's only about a forty-five-foot drop. Today it's closer to sixty-five. Its length has been known to reach around seventy."

Waterfall. Feet. Who cares? Hadn't they almost kissed? *Maybe I should jump in and over the falls. Perhaps then he'd notice me.* "Interesting," she responded.

"Come on." He grabbed her hand and led her deeper into the woods.

"Where are we going?" She huffed, trying to keep pace with him. His long legs spanned three times the distance of hers.

"There's a spot up this trail that overlooks the falls. It's simply majestic."

"What about Urias?"

"He'll be fine. We won't stay too late. They say there is only one other place in the world that has a moonbow. It's this most incredible sight. I'm sorry you won't get to see it tonight."

"All right." She felt like Ruth about to say, "Where you lead, I will follow." But quoting Scripture, or what she remembered of Scripture, with this man seemed risky at best.

He led them through a natural tunnel maybe five feet in length. Its darkness sent a wave of caution through her.

"Mac, perhaps we should stay closer to the falls in case Urias needs us."

He stopped and turned before she realized it. Smack. She plowed into his chest. "Sorry." She placed her hands on his chest to push herself back.

Mac placed his hands over hers. "My mistake." He caressed the top of her hands with his.

She looked up into his deep blue eyes. She'd noticed before how they differed from her own. A darker shade. His heart beat strong and vibrant under her hands.

Mac cleared his throat. "I think you're right. We should get back."

Back? Back where? She didn't want to move. Squeezing her eyes closed, she took in a deep breath and stepped away. Perhaps it was time for her to sit in the river. How could one man make her forget all her common sense and sensibilities? *Lord, give me strength.*

❧

They walked back to the overlook in silence. Twice tonight he'd been about to kiss her. *Twice. Am I so weak, Lord?* "Pamela?"

"Hmm?" Her voice alone stirred up sweet images.

How could he ask a widow to court him in a year after she mourned the death of her husband? A year he figured would be a fair amount of time. He could manage a year. He hoped.

"If all goes well, we should get to Creelsboro in a week. We've traveled just about half the distance. If I took you there by the river, we could be there in three days. But I can't imagine trying to float this wagon down the Cumberland." Conversation was better than letting his thoughts carry on.

"I could go down to three, possibly two, trunks."

Mac smiled. "My canoe isn't that large."

"Oh."

"We can drive the wagon. There will be fewer taverns,

though. At this point we fork off from the Wilderness Road and head west on far less constructed trails. It'll be rough going in some spots."

"I'm sorry. I've been such a— Oh my, that's beautiful," Pamela exclaimed.

Mac turned. A large bird swooped over the waterfall.

She shivered as the crisp night air breezed past. He positioned his body to block the wind for her.

"Thank you."

"You're welcome."

He smiled. "Pamela, have you thought about our conversation regarding Indian charms, omens, and such?"

She nodded her head and looked down at her feet. "I'm not as strong as you. I know you're right, but so much has happened in the past. I don't know what to believe anymore."

"Believe in truth, God's truth, the Bible. The strength of those words is so much stronger than anything man can offer."

Her glance caught his. She turned and looked back at the falls.

"Pam." He placed his hand on her shoulder. "Death is always around us. But life is as well—abundant, radiant life. Like the moon, it's a reflection of light. It isn't the real light that comes from the sun. God loves you, Pam. He aches when you ache. He knows your losses, your hurts, and He knows your joys, your loves, and many other blessings He gives us. Trust Him, Pam, not a piece of stone or some water-soaked tealeaves. Trust real life, abundant life. Trust in Him."

She turned in his arms. Tears streamed down her cheeks. "I want to, Mac, I really do."

Gently he brushed away her tears. Her skin was so soft and velvety against his. His heart pounded in his chest. Slipping his fingers through her golden strands, he groaned and pulled her toward him.

She didn't resist. Her delicate pink lips parted slightly. Slowly his descended upon hers. They tasted like fine honey. He deepened the kiss, pulling her closer and wrapping her protectively in his arms.

She placed her hands upon his chest and pushed back slightly. "Oh, Mac," she whispered, her voice shaky.

"Sor—"

She reached up and pulled his head back down. The kiss lingered. All thoughts, the sound of the rushing water, disappeared. It was just the two of them wrapped in each other's arms, savoring each other's kiss.

Then she pulled back. She trembled in his arms. "I'm sorry. I. . .we. . .shouldn't have done that."

How could she say such a thing? How could she think it? Then his clouded mind began to clear. Her husband hadn't even been gone for two weeks, and here he was kissing her senseless. "I'm sorry, Mrs. Danner. I promise it won't happen again."

"No, Mac. It's not what you're thinking."

"Pamela, I know you're vulnerable right now. I've taken advantage, and I shouldn't have. Forgive me. I don't know what came over me."

"Forgive you? No, Mac. It isn't you. It's me."

He placed his forefinger to her tender lips. "Shh, it's not you. It's me. I'm the man, I'm older, I know better."

"What does that have to do with anything? You and I both know what just happened, and it had nothing to do with you being a man and being older. Wait a minute, I didn't mean that. It did have something to do with you being a man, of course, but. . ."

He loved it when she was riled up. He loved the fire in her eyes, the bright pink that flamed her cheeks. A miscreant smile slid up his cheek.

"I'm a widower, too. I understand these emotions right after your spouse dies. It's my fault."

She placed her hands on her hips. "If my excuse for having kissed you is because I'm missing my husband, what's your justification?"

"I don't know, a moment of weakness on my part. I assure you it won't happen again. A gentleman should never behave in such a manner."

"A gentleman? Since when are you a gentleman?"

"Don't push me, Pamela. I've apologized. Let's just leave it at that."

Mac turned and stomped back toward their campsite. He foolishly had given in to his desires, and now he'd never have an opportunity to ask her formally to court him.

❧

Pamela sat down on the rock and huddled into herself. *Why'd I have to goad the man, Lord? And what's this big deal about whose fault it was? We were both guilty. We both wanted it. I should have told him right then I wasn't married to Quinton, that he's my brother. But he got me so riled up pretending to take full responsibility. Since when is a woman not responsible for her own actions?*

Taking in deeper, more calming breaths, she closed her eyes. "He's right about one thing, Lord. I either trust You or I don't." She took the Indian fetish from her pocket and tossed it into the pool below.

"Father, give me strength. Help me tell Mac the truth." She heard a rustle in the undergrowth behind her. Pamela jumped up and returned to their campsite. Mac and Urias were both in the tent. She would sleep in the wagon. Tonight would be her first night alone under the stars since Quinton's untimely death. Knowing Mac was a shout away didn't ease her worries or concerns. Memories of the bear jumping out of the wagon didn't help, either.

Once in bed, she found no rest. Images and emotions repeated over and over again in her mind. Did she truly love Mac, or was she just enamored with him? Pamela rolled to her side and moaned into her pillow. For hours she kept seeing those images, feeling those strong emotions that drew her to him. Every time she pictured herself telling him the truth, he'd storm off.

Unable to sleep, she went back to the waterfall. The water cascading over the rocky cliff drew her. She felt the cleansing work of God near the water's edge. "Father, forgive me. I've been such a fool. I've allowed men's foolish thoughts to interfere with the truth of Your Word."

Pouring her heart out to God, Pamela continued to repent for her past sins, her lack of faith, and for the foolish lies she'd been saying to keep Mac from learning the truth about her relationship with Quinton.

Tears of joy streamed down her face. For the first time in her life, she felt the peace of God. She opened her eyes and saw the heavens on fire. She blinked. Stunned, she stayed on her knees.

She screamed. "Dear Jesus, what have I done now?"

sixteen

The heavens blazed with fire. Stars burned as they plummeted toward the earth. *Is it Judgment Day?* Mac scrambled from the tent and ran to the wagon. He had to make things right with Pamela.

She wasn't there.

"Dear Lord, where is she?" He raced back to the waterfall. His heart pounded with excitement and nervous energy. So many stars fell from the heavens it appeared to be day. But he knew it couldn't be. The sky itself remained black.

Pamela was on her knees overlooking the waterfall.

"Thank You, Lord," Mac whispered.

"Pam," he shouted.

There was no response. She couldn't hear him over the rushing waters. He came a bit closer, moving more slowly. He heard her crying. She appeared to be weaving back and forth.

"Pamela," he called again.

She turned, jumped up, and ran to him. "Oh, Mac. I am so sorry. I was wrong, so very wrong. And now the end of the world has come and you'll never know."

He opened his arms, and she collapsed into them. "It's not the end of the world." He glanced back up at the sky. "Perhaps it is. But nothing can be that bad."

"I lied, Mac. I lied to you. I'm not who you think I am."

"What? You're not Pamela Danner?"

"No, I mean, yes, I am but. . .oh, Mac, I'm so scared. I was praying to God, asking for forgiveness for my life, for lying to you, for everything I've ever done wrong. And when I opened my eyes, the heavens were on fire. I'm such a

153

wretched person. I've insulted God."

"Shh, please slow down and tell me what this is all about." Mac cradled her protectively in his embrace.

He watched as thousands of stars burned long white trails across the sky and continued to fall at an incredible rate. Objectively, he knew she couldn't have sinned so much that her mere confession would set the heavens ablaze, but he couldn't help wondering what she had done to believe she had.

Yet if this was the sign of the return of Christ, how much time on earth did he have left? And why should anyone's sins against him matter? Thankful he'd spent some time with the Lord the previous morning, he knew he had little to repent for. Little, except for the kiss he'd shared with Pamela a few hours ago. Mac fired off another prayer, asking for the Lord's forgiveness.

"Come on," he said gently to Pamela, "let's check on Urias. If one of those fireballs hits, I don't want him to be caught unaware."

She followed in silence. He wondered if she were going into some kind of shock. Not that he wasn't on the border of it himself. Never had he seen anything like this before. The scent of sulfur hung in the air. Was this the hellfire and brimstone some preachers spoke of?

At the campsite Pamela again fell to her knees and continued her silent pleading with God. What had this woman done? And what did she mean by she wasn't who he thought her to be?

The money. He eyed her cautiously. Was she a bank robber? Or worse? Had she caused the wagon to roll and kill her husband? No, that wasn't it. She wasn't that kind of person. She had too much compassion and too much fear to be that brutal. What could she possibly have done that kept her on her knees crying before God?

Father, am I so full of pride that I can't see my own sins?

Should I be on my knees repenting? He searched his heart and knew he was free of the guilt of Tilly's death. Daily repentance kept him right before God. Pamela, on the other hand, did have mixed-up views of God. And her beliefs in omens and superstitions were definitely not healthy. *Lord, I know I'm not perfect, but I am content in my relationship with You. I have peace; I'm not afraid.*

Reaching the tent, Mac entered and nudged the boy's shoulder. "Urias, wake up."

"Huh?" A lump of red curls rose from the bedroll.

"The heavens are on fire. You best get right with God, Son. I think it might just be the end of the world."

"What?" Urias stuck a finger in his ear and wiggled it.

"Look." Mac flung aside the tent flap and exposed the brilliant view.

"The sky is on fire."

Mac grinned. "That is my point. Come on; join Pamela and me. I'm afraid one of these fireballs might hit the wagon or tent."

Urias scrambled for his pants and hiked them up as he stumbled out of the tent. "I swear, I didn't do nothin'."

"Look, I'm not one to force my religion on anyone, but the Bible says in Mark 13:25 that when Jesus comes again, 'the stars of heaven shall fall, and the powers that are in heaven shall be shaken.' The choice is yours."

Urias's eyes widened. "What can I do?"

"Pray, pray like you never have. If this is the end of the world, time is short."

Urias knelt down near Pam and silently pleaded with God.

Mac knelt beside him and praised God. *Father, forgive me for forcing the boy. If this isn't right, help me love him into the kingdom. I just don't want to see him go to hell.*

After prayers, they all gathered together and sat in silence, watching the heavens burn. Mac kept wondering why he was still here. If this was the end of the world, why hadn't anything happened? Where was God, and why were they still sitting on earth?

"Mac." Pamela's voice cracked.

They'd been watching for hours.

"I'm not a widow. Quinton was my brother."

"What?"

"Quinton was my brother. We weren't married."

Anger welled up within him. She'd lied. She did say she had a brother, but. . . He'd felt so guilty for kissing a recently widowed woman, only to discover now that she wasn't a widow. "But you said—"

"I never said he was my husband. You said it. I simply didn't correct the mistake. I didn't know you. I feared for my safety. A man was more than likely going to give a woman more sympathy for being a widow than a–a. . ."

Mac took in a deep breath. She'd deceived him for her own selfish reasons, and he'd fallen into her trap. Just as he had for Tilly. *What kind of fool am I?*

"Fine," he said, cutting her off. "You repented. It's between you and God, not me."

"I'm sorry." She left Mac and Urias and returned to the wagon as the last of the fiery missiles streaked across the blackness.

≈

Pamela snuggled under the covers. Fear over the past couple hours had exhausted her. Finally, Mac knew the truth. But the pain she'd seen in his eyes—Tilly had deceived him, and he'd married her. She knew he felt the same sting from her own omission.

≈

The next few days went by in silence. Urias wasn't too sure about his forced prayer to give himself to God. Mac barely spoke a word. And Pamela listened to other travelers speaking about the night it rained fire. Many, like Urias, had confessed their sins and accepted salvation due to fear. If she was grateful for anything, it was that she'd confessed her sins before the stars burned.

They reached Jamestown in five days. Mac's parents willingly opened their home to Pamela and Urias. She wondered if she could travel the next two days to Creelsboro on her own. Or possibly hook up with another group of travelers heading down there. Of course, Mac wouldn't hear of such a thing. He still took his oath to Quinton seriously, and no matter what his feelings might be about her, he'd fulfill his promise. Pam knew that in the depths of her heart. She ached for Mac. She wasn't like Tilly, at least she hadn't meant to be. The closer she came to Creelsboro, the more she didn't want to go. Her father's dream had become her nightmare. Where would she ever find peace?

Pam worked her way toward the woods behind the farmhouse. She needed time to think. The dry, empty fields ready for planting next spring reminded her of how empty her own heart was. She'd fallen in love with a man who could never love her because she'd deceived him. There had been peace, comfort, a sense of belonging when she was wrapped in Mac's arms. Now, she'd never know that peace again, unless. . .

She eyed the large farmhouse. She thought about her experiences on the trail the past five days. They'd been long and hard. When Mac had said the road wouldn't be as nice as the Wilderness Road, he hadn't been fooling. Mac had taken to running again. He had let Urias and herself ride the wagon. He claimed he needed to keep his muscles in shape or he wouldn't be able to get back to his winter cabin before the severe storms hit.

The image of the rugged mountain man dressed in his leathers, running ahead of them or beside them, sent chills down her spine. His long black hair danced on his shoulders as he stepped with a perfect beat. "God, what can I do to show him I'm not like Tilly?"

"Hello," a gentle feminine voice called from behind Pam.

She closed her eyes, took in a deep breath, and turned to face Mac's mother. "Mrs. MacKenneth. I'm sorry, I didn't hear you come up." Had Mac learned that trait from his mother?

"When I'm lost in thought, I often don't hear so well. Nash has told me about your losses. I'm sorry."

Nash? Oh, right, Mac's first name. He seemed more like a Mac than a Nash. "Thank you."

"He's also been telling me about this young boy you two rescued on the road. He says you've offered him a job at your store."

"Ah, yes. Mac also invited Urias to come and live with him," Pamela replied.

"Forgive me for being forward, Dear, but why would you want to take on the responsibility?"

Pamela didn't know anymore. "I like the boy, and I thought I could help him receive an education. He isn't able to read, you know. He thinks he's hidden it from us, but I've seen the signs before."

"I taught my children at home."

Pamela smiled. She'd wondered where Mac had received his education. "You were a good teacher."

"Nash always had a way with books and learning. Betsy, well, she couldn't be bothered with it. Lisa loved to read, but numbers. . .she just never got the hang of them." Mac's mother motioned to the space on the bench beside Pamela. "May I?"

Pamela slid over. "Of course."

"My dear, if I'm being nosy, just tell me, but what happened between you and Nash?"

Pamela kneaded her hands in her lap. "Nothing, we just

sort of grated against each other from the start."

Mrs. MacKenneth looked down her pencil-straight nose and raised her eyebrows.

"It didn't help that I lied to him," Pam added.

"Ah, about your being married."

She nodded. "I never really said I was married to Quinton. Mac assumed it, and I just felt I was safer if he believed I was a widow. Is that so wrong? A woman alone in the wilderness with nothing more than a tall mountain man looming over me?"

Mrs. MacKenneth chuckled. "I see your point. But once you knew you could trust him, shouldn't you have told him the truth?"

"I tried, but every time something came up or we'd argue about something else. Begging your pardon, Mrs. Mac-Kenneth, but your son can be a pretty obstinate man."

The older woman patted Pamela's knee. "Oh, I seem to know a little about that. Tilly didn't understand that, and she pushed and pushed Nash. He's never talked much about what happened between the two of them, but something happened on his trip here with you. He's finally released the guilt he's carried for so long."

A loud clanging noise echoed in Pamela's ear. Mrs. Mac-Kenneth jumped up and ran toward the house. "Emergency," she hollered.

❧

Mac laid his father on his bed. "I'll get the doctor."

"What's wrong?" His mother's voice shook as she glanced through her bedroom doorway.

"Dad's hurt. I think he might have broken a hip. I'm going to get the doctor. I'll be back as soon as I can." He slipped on his coonskin cap and within two strides was out the front door.

"What's the matter?" Pamela asked, huffing. Catching her wind, she braced herself against the porch railing.

"Father's had an accident. I'm getting the doctor. Help my mother." Mac jumped off the porch. "Please."

He ran toward the center of town. Finding the doctor at his home had been an answer to prayer. Within seconds they were in the doctor's carriage and speeding back to the farmhouse.

Hours later, Mac had some memory of telling the doctor all he knew about the accident, but when he found himself pacing the front porch, he had no true memory of the event. Had he dreamed it? Was it real? Had the accident even happened?

The front door opened with a creak. "Doc, how is he?" Mac asked. Everyone gathered around the doctor.

"His hip is broken. You called it right. Hopefully it will mend well. He'll need to stay off it for weeks."

Mac nodded. He would make certain his father stayed down. "Thank you."

"You're welcome. Sorry I couldn't give you better news. I've set the bones in place as best I could, but it's up to the good Lord to bring healing in a joint like that."

Mac swallowed the lump in his throat. He couldn't picture his father an invalid. The man hadn't been sick a day in his life except for a sniffle now and again. "I'll take care of him."

"You do that, Son. I best get going. The missus baked me an apple pie, and all that good cooking in your kitchen got my stomach a-churning. Good night, Mac."

"Night, Doc."

Urias stood beside him. "Does this mean we won't be going to your cabin in the gap?"

"Afraid so."

"What about bringing Mrs., I mean, Miss Danner to Creelsboro?"

The point of Pamela not being Mrs. Danner still stuck in the pit of his stomach. "Tell the folks I'll be back shortly."

"But, what about—"

"Later." Mac ran off again, this time to the neighbor's

farm. If anyone could be trusted to take Pamela Danner to Creelsboro, it was Tanner James, his childhood friend and neighbor.

Thirty minutes later he stood on Tanner's front porch, explaining the situation. After a quick handshake, the men parted. Tanner would take Pamela Danner to Creelsboro in the morning. Urias would join them, and the boy would then decide where he wanted to live.

Mac reached the farm about dusk. The dim light from the oil lamps glowed, welcoming him home.

"Nash, your father's been asking to see you." His mother wrapped her soft, cuddly arms around him.

"How is he?"

"In a lot of pain, but the medication the doctor gave him has been helping."

Pain medication. His father would never take the stuff unless he was in agony. Mac released his mother and went to his parents' room. His father lay motionless on the bed. This once-vibrant man appeared weak. Mac's stomach tightened. Beside the bed, a lone chair stood. He knew his mother had kept it warm since the accident. He sat down and prayed.

"Nash," his father croaked. "I'm glad you're here, Son. I'll need you to take care of the farm."

"You know I will. I've asked Tanner to take Miss Danner to Creelsboro."

His father gripped his hand and gave it a gentle squeeze. "Thank you. God brought you home at the right time, Son."

Mac smiled. "Yeah, I believe He did. Rest, Father. I'll see you in the morning."

His father nodded his sparsely covered head, then closed his eyes.

Mac got up to leave the room and found Pamela in the doorway with a tray of food. No doubt she'd overheard the news that he wouldn't be taking her to Creelsboro.

"I thought you might like to have something to eat while you visited with your father," she said.

He reached for the tray. "Thank you. I'll eat in the kitchen."

She nibbled her lower lip. "I take it I leave in the morning?"

"Yes. I've asked Tanner James to escort you to Creelsboro. He's a good man. I've known him since I was five. You can trust him. And he knows you're not a widow."

She pursed her lips.

Mac sighed. "Sorry, that was uncalled for. I'm tired, and I have a lot on my mind."

"I'll go pack." Pamela retreated down the hallway, the hem of her skirt fluttering out behind her.

Tomorrow couldn't come soon enough. Every time he saw her, he wanted to wrap her in his arms. But he'd been a fool once, and he wasn't about to be a fool again. Tilly had taken every ounce of trust he had in the opposite sex and thrown it away. Pamela was no different. She was a liar, too. He had to keep reminding himself of that. It was the only sane thing to do.

He set the tray on the kitchen table and removed the pie tin she'd placed over his plate. The aroma made his stomach gurgle. Unlike Tilly, the woman could cook. Bowing his head, he said a prayer of thanks and asked the Lord to give Pamela safe passage to Creelsboro.

The next morning he found himself up early milking the cows, tending the chickens, feeding the livestock. Tanner and his wife, Elsa, drove over in their wagon. After brief introductions, he waved Tanner, Pamela, and Urias on their way to Creelsboro. Elsa returned to her farm.

Later Mac found himself in the barn. He noticed lots of little things that were out of place, partially finished. His father was slowing down. Perhaps the time had come for him to stay in Jamestown and take over the farm.

seventeen

Creelsboro was a small town full of people. More people traveled through the area than actually lived there, Pamela had observed over the past two months. She had finally decided to put the store up for sale and hoped to return home to Virginia in the spring.

If she'd learned anything over the past several weeks, it had been that she didn't belong in Creelsboro, never had. Quinton would have thrived here. But Pam knew she could never enjoy it. Marriage proposals came daily from men heading west. The other merchants didn't take her seriously until they needed some of her stock.

She'd set up a system of regular shipments of supplies that kept her store well stocked. The prices she could charge for items were practically criminal. But there was no joy in turning a profit. Her mind continued to replay the events of November thirteenth, the night it rained fire. The night she fell in love and lost him.

People still spoke of that night. Some folks had started attending church services after their hurried confessions. At recent Sunday services, however, she'd noticed the congregation thinning. Thankfully, her confession had not brought down the heavens. But the fear of that moment still struck deep in her heart as a reminder to stay right with the Lord and not fall into the silly notions she had been so easily swayed by.

News was spreading of a scientist, Denison Olmsted, and his findings about the meteor shower. He claimed folks from Boston to Ohio had seen the incredible display. He also said it would be seen again—that the meteors were from a cloud in space. Pamela wouldn't argue the man's findings; they seemed logical. She only knew that God had used that night to set her on the right track with Him. That she didn't need to live in fear of the elemental spirits of this world, as Mac had pointed out.

The thought of moving back home to Virginia where she had friends and neighbors was her only refuge. Living alone in a settlement full of men brought an even greater sense of loneliness. She knew she could never love another man as deeply as she loved Mac.

The bell above the door jangled. Pam glanced over. "Urias." She smiled.

"Hi, Miss Danner. How are you?"

"Fine, fine. Tell me, what brought you down to Creelsboro? You look like you've grown a couple inches. What are they feeding you on that farm?"

Urias grinned and stuffed his thumbs behind his suspenders. "Lots. But it's hard work, and Mrs. MacKenneth insists on my schoolin'. She taught Mac, ya know."

"I know." Pam opened her arms. "Come here; give me a hug. I've missed you."

Urias bounced over the counter and gave her a bear hug.

"How's Mr. MacKenneth? Mac's dad," she qualified. She didn't want Urias to think she was asking about Mac. Not that she didn't want to know, longed to know, how he was doing.

The boy hoisted himself up on the counter. "Doing good. He's gettin' around with a couple canes now."

"That's wonderful. I've prayed for him often."

Urias smiled.

"What did you say brought you down here?"

"Supplies." Urias crossed his arms and looked around. "Not bad. You own all this?"

"For a little while. I'm selling it and moving back East."

"Why? I mean, after all it took to get here."

"It's a long story really, but I never wanted to move here. It was my father's dream and my brother's."

Urias nodded his head and nibbled his inner cheek.

"Do you have a list for the supplies you need?"

"Oh, sorry. Nope. Mac's gettin' 'em."

"Oh." Obviously Mac didn't want to see her. It didn't matter that she ached to see him.

The bell on the doorjamb jingled. A blast of cold air filled the room.

"Parson Kincaid, what can I do for you?"

He removed his black hat and folded it in his hands. The thin, middle-aged man was dressed in black from head to toe except for the backward collar of white. "Miss Danner, there is a reason for you to come to the church."

Pamela placed her hand on the counter, bracing herself. What could she have done wrong? "What's the matter?"

"Truthfully, I've never heard of such a thing. But the gentleman insists."

"Parson, is everything all right?"

"Honestly, I'm not sure. In all my years, I've never seen it done this way."

Curiosity was definitely getting the best of her. "All right. Let me gather my coat."

Parson Kincaid nodded his head and placed his hat back upon it. Pamela slipped to the back room and retrieved her wool coat.

Urias stood by the parson. "Would you like me to come?" His freckled face didn't hold the same joy it had moments before.

Perhaps it was wise to have him with her. Not that she couldn't trust Parson Kincaid. He and his wife, Martha, had shown her great kindness over the past couple months. He'd helped her understand that repentance freed her from God's judgment, that she didn't have to live in fear.

"Sure." She slipped the key from the folds of her apron, locking the door after they all exited.

They walked in silence across the hard, rutted street. Winter frost lined the tops of the ruts. When they entered the church, she found it warm and comfortable. "Go to the altar," the parson instructed. "There's a message for you there."

She opened her mouth to speak. He smiled and placed a hand on Urias's shoulder. "You'll need a few minutes. I'll keep the boy with me. Holler if you need me."

Pamela's insides quivered like a new fawn trying to stand on its legs for the first time. Working her way down the center aisle, she approached the small oak table with white painted sides and a dark stained top. Carved on the front panel were the words "Remember Me." She closed her eyes, knowing the words were Christ's regarding communion. On top of the table a small oval of white lace accented a small circle of gold. A rolled-up piece of paper rested within the band.

Her hands trembled.

She reached for the band and pulled out the paper. Unfurling the note, she read the words, "Forgive me."

❧

Mac stood in the shadowed room off to the side of the altar. Pamela dropped the note and braced herself, holding the edges of the table. With her head bent, she asked, "Where are you, Mac?"

Closing the distance between them, he silently stood behind her. "Right here," he whispered. A whiff of her delicate perfume tickled his nostrils. "I've missed you."

"I don't understand." Her profiled body held fast, not turning around to face him. Her knuckles whitened.

Father, help me say the right words here. "I'm sorry for not giving you a chance to speak. Mother's made it abundantly clear that I was rather hardheaded."

A gentle smirk rose on her pink lips.

"Please, forgive me, Pamela. I held against you what Tilly had done to me. It wasn't right, and it wasn't fair. I can't blame you for being afraid in a wilderness area with no one to trust. And most importantly, with Jasper hot on your trail. I assumed you were Quinton's widow. Your decision to simply let me continue with that misimpression was no different from my choice to let Jasper think we were married."

Her body trembled.

He ached to close the distance between them but didn't dare.

She squeezed her eyes tighter. "I loved you," she confessed. "You hurt me."

He took the final step that remained between them. He could feel the heat from her body. Still she remained resolute, not wavering.

"I'm sorry." He dropped to his knees and placed a hand over hers.

"Why didn't you come to the store? Why haven't you tried to contact me? A letter, a message, something. . .I don't understand. You couldn't get rid of me fast enough." She turned and looked down at him.

"I wanted to. I really did. But I didn't know how. I've been praying and waiting. Honey, the waiting has been the hardest part. I wanted to come before now. But Father needed me. The farm couldn't be left unattended for that long a period. I even thought of sending Urias. But God said no. He said to wait. I love you, Pamela. I know it seems rather late to say that, but I do with all my heart. I never thought I could love another woman. I put myself in an area where few women lived. And the ones who were nearby were married. I tried, I really tried to avoid women. But God had other plans. I know that now. But I fought Him every step of the way."

Tears fell down her face.

Mac stood and pulled her close. "I'm so sorry. I love you. I want us to be together. I've even arranged for us to be married."

She placed her hands on his chest and pushed out of his embrace. "You what? This ring is for today?"

He looked down and scuffed the floor with his right foot. "Uh, yeah."

"You are really something, Mac. You come into my life and expect me to just drop everything and go running off with you." She placed her hands on her hips. "I have responsibilities, you know. I guess you expected me to just marry you and ride off into the sunset, forgetting any responsibility I might have."

That had been the plan. It had sounded good before he heard it from her lips. Now he wasn't too sure. "Yeah."

A whistle went streaming through her teeth. "Have you heard of courting?"

"Yes, but. . ." How could he word this without losing her?

"Mac, there's a lot we have to know about each other before we talk marriage."

"Like what?" He sat down on the front pew. She came up beside him and sat down.

"I don't know. But we don't know each other all that well."

"We traveled together for almost three weeks, isn't that enough?" His voice rose.

"Shh," Pam admonished and placed her hand upon his.

This is not going the way I had planned. He sighed.

"Mac, I. . ."

He turned, embracing her, and captured her lips.

She moaned. *Or was that him?*

Pulling away, she gasped, "Mac, stop."

"I love you, Pam. I want you."

"I love you, too, but. . ."

Joy filled him. He placed his finger to her lips. "Don't, not just yet. Let me enjoy what you just said."

Pamela shook her head from side to side and laughed. "It wouldn't be boring."

"What?"

"Marriage to you."

"Please, Pamela. Please marry me. I brought Mother and Urias as witnesses. I even convinced Parson Kincaid that you'd agree."

"No, Mac. Not here, not now. Not like this."

"I don't understand." He slumped back into the pew.

"Let me try to explain. I have a business. Are you planning on staying in Creelsboro?"

"No, I thought you'd come back to the farm with me. I know you didn't want the business."

"You're right. I don't, and I've put it on the market."

"See." He felt like a little boy.

"See what? That I should be irresponsible and just lock up the business and not sell it first?"

"It'll sell."

"Yes, it will. But if I simply closed the store, I'd lose money on the sale. I'm certain you are aware that an active, successful business is worth far more than a closed one."

"I don't care about money."

Pamela chuckled. "I know. And I'm not as concerned as you think. But I do believe the Bible tells us to be good stewards of what we have. And I don't believe it's being a good steward to simply walk away from one's obligations. In the same way that you couldn't walk away from your father's need for you on the farm."

"Very well, you've made your point. But I still want to get married."

Pamela chuckled. Seeing Mac pout sent an image of a young boy, their son, and how he would behave in years to come. "I do, too," she confessed.

"Yahoo!" he shouted. "You mean it?"

"Yes. But not today."

"When?"

"In time. A woman needs to plan her wedding, make her dress, prepare, you know?"

"Honey, I don't understand women all that well. You, for one, know that. But if you need time, I can wait."

"Mac, where will we live? On the farm? In the wilderness? Where?"

"The farm. Dad will never be able to run it again. He'll get around and all, but he won't have the strength. However, we'll need to take a trip back to my cabin in the gap. There are some items I'd like to keep." He leaned up beside her. "I thought we could make it a romantic getaway for just the two of us."

"Oh, Mac." She threw herself into his arms and kissed him. "I'd love that. There is one thing you should know." She whispered into his ear.

"You traveled with that much?" His eyes bulged.

"Yes. Can you handle the dowry?"

"I guess. What are we going to do with that kind of money?"

"Building our own private house might be nice."

Mac laughed. "Anything you'd like. Just promise me you'll marry me?"

"I promise." His sweet lips were upon hers before she could say another thing. *Thank You, Lord, for the night it rained fire.*

A Letter To Our Readers

Dear Reader:

In order that we might better contribute to your reading enjoyment, we would appreciate your taking a few minutes to respond to the following questions. We welcome your comments and read each form and letter we receive. When completed, please return to the following:

Fiction Editor
Heartsong Presents
PO Box 719
Uhrichsville, Ohio 44683

1. Did you enjoy reading *Raining Fire* by Lynn A. Coleman?
   ❑ Very much! I would like to see more books by this author!
   ❑ Moderately. I would have enjoyed it more if

   _____

   _____

   _____

2. Are you a member of **Heartsong Presents**? ❑ Yes ❑ No
   If no, where did you purchase this book? _____

   _____

3. How would you rate, on a scale from 1 (poor) to 5 (superior), the cover design? _____

4. On a scale from 1 (poor) to 10 (superior), please rate the following elements.

   ____ Heroine   ____ Plot
   ____ Hero   ____ Inspirational theme
   ____ Setting   ____ Secondary characters

6. How has this book inspired your life?_____
_____
_____

7. What settings would you like to see covered in future
   Heartsong Presents books? _____
_____
_____

8. What are some inspirational themes you would like to see
   treated in future books? _____
_____
_____

9. Would you be interested in reading other **Heartsong
   Presents** titles?   ❏ Yes   ❏ No

10. Please check your age range:
     ❏ Under 18   ❏ 18-24
     ❏ 25-34   ❏ 35-45
     ❏ 46-55   ❏ Over 55

Name_____
Occupation _____
Address _____
City_____ State_____ Zip_____
E-mail_____

Ohio

*T*he first decade of the nineteenth century is full of promise and adventure for the infant state of Ohio. But for the three Carson sisters, it is filled with trepidation as they struggle with the loss of their parents in the battle for statehood.

What will be Kate, Annabelle, and Claire's legacy of faith and love for following generations?

Historical, paperback, 480 pages, 5 ³/₁₆" x 8"

♥ ♥ ♥ ♥ ♥ ♥ ♥ ♥ ♥ ♥ ♥ ♥ ♥ ♥ ♥ ♥ ♥

Please send me _____ copies of *Ohio*. I am enclosing $6.99 for each.
(Please add $2.00 to cover postage and handling per order. OH add 6% tax.)

Send check or money order, no cash or C.O.D.s please.

Name_____

Address _____

City, State, Zip _____

To place a credit card order, call 1-800-847-8270.
Send to: Heartsong Presents Reader Service, PO Box 721, Uhrichsville, OH 44683

♥ ♥ ♥ ♥ ♥ ♥ ♥ ♥ ♥ ♥ ♥ ♥ ♥ ♥ ♥ ♥ ♥

Heartsong

HISTORICAL ROMANCE IS CHEAPER BY THE DOZEN!

Buy any assortment of twelve *Heartsong Presents* titles and save 25% off of the already discounted price of $3.25 each!

Any 12 Heartsong Presents titles for only $30.00*

*plus $2.00 shipping and handling per order and sales tax where applicable.

HEARTSONG PRESENTS TITLES AVAILABLE NOW:

___HP179 *Her Father's Love*, N. Lavo	T. Shuttlesworth
___HP180 *Friend of a Friend*, J. Richardson	___HP319 *Margaret's Quest*, M. Chapman
___HP183 *A New Love*, V. Wiggins	___HP320 *Hope in the Great Southland*, M. Hawkins
___HP184 *The Hope That Sings*, J. A. Grote	
___HP195 *Come Away My Love*, T. Peterson	___HP323 *No More Sea*, G. Brandt
___HP203 *Ample Portions*, D. L. Christner	___HP324 *Love in the Great Southland*, M. Hawkins
___HP208 *Love's Tender Path*, B. L. Etchison	
___HP212 *Crosswinds*, S. Rohde	___HP327 *Plains of Promise*, C. Coble
___HP215 *Tulsa Trespass*, N. J. Lutz	___HP331 *A Man for Libby*, J. A. Grote
___HP216 *Black Hawk's Feather*, C. Scheidies	___HP332 *Hidden Trails*, J. B. Schneider
___HP219 *A Heart for Home*, N. Morris	___HP339 *Birdsong Road*, M. L. Colln
___HP223 *Threads of Love*, J. M. Miller	___HP340 *Lone Wolf*, L. Lough
___HP224 *Edge of Destiny*, D. Mindrup	___HP343 *Texas Rose*, D. W. Smith
___HP227 *Bridget's Bargain*, L. Lough	___HP344 *The Measure of a Man*, C. Cox
___HP228 *Falling Water Valley*, M. L. Colln	___HP351 *Courtin' Patience*, K. Comeaux
___HP235 *The Lady Rose*, J. Williams	___HP352 *After the Flowers Fade*, A. Rognlie
___HP236 *Valiant Heart*, S. Laity	___HP356 *Texas Lady*, D. W. Smith
___HP239 *Logan's Lady*, T. Peterson	___HP363 *Rebellious Heart*, R. Druten
___HP240 *The Sun Still Shines*, L. Ford	___HP371 *Storm*, D. L. Christner
___HP243 *The Rising Son*, D. Mindrup	___HP372 *'Til We Meet Again*, P. Griffin
___HP247 *Strong as the Redwood*, K. Billerbeck	___HP380 *Neither Bond Nor Free*, N. C. Pykare
___HP248 *Return to Tulsa*, N. J. Lutz	___HP384 *Texas Angel*, D. W. Smith
___HP259 *Five Geese Flying*, T. Peterson	___HP387 *Grant Me Mercy*, J. Stengl
___HP260 *The Will and the Way*, D. Pace	___HP388 *Lessons in Love*, N. Lavo
___HP263 *The Starfire Quilt*, A. Allen	___HP392 *Healing Sarah's Heart*, T. Shuttlesworth
___HP264 *Journey Toward Home*, C. Cox	
___HP271 *Where Leads the Heart*, C. Coble	___HP395 *To Love a Stranger*, C. Coble
___HP272 *Albert's Destiny*, B. L. Etchison	___HP400 *Susannah's Secret*, K. Comeaux
___HP275 *Along Unfamiliar Paths*, A. Rognlie	___HP403 *The Best Laid Plans*, C. M. Parker
___HP279 *An Unexpected Love*, A. Boeshaar	___HP407 *Sleigh Bells*, J. M. Miller
___HP299 *Em's Only Chance*, R. Dow	___HP408 *Destinations*, T. H. Murray
___HP300 *Changes of the Heart*, J. M. Miller	___HP411 *Spirit of the Eagle*, G. Fields
___HP303 *Maid of Honor*, C. R. Scheidies	___HP412 *To See His Way*, K. Paul
___HP304 *Song of the Cimarron*, K. Stevens	___HP415 *Sonoran Sunrise*, N. J. Farrier
___HP307 *Silent Stranger*, P. Darty	___HP416 *Both Sides of the Easel*, B. Youree
___HP308 *A Different Kind of Heaven*,	___HP419 *Captive Heart*, D. Mindrup
	___HP420 *In the Secret Place*, P. Griffin

(If ordering from this page, please remember to include it with the order form.)

Presents

Great Inspirational Romance at a Great Price!

Heartsong Presents books are inspirational romances in contemporary and historical settings, designed to give you an enjoyable, spirit-lifting reading experience. You can choose wonderfully written titles from some of today's best authors like Peggy Darty, Sally Laity, Tracie Peterson, Colleen L. Reece, Debra White Smith, and many others.

When ordering quantities less than twelve, above titles are $3.25 each.
Not all titles may be available at time of order.